P

PE

Tam Hoskyns has worked
She and her family live in L *The Talking Cure*,
is also published in Penguin.

TAM HOSKYNS

PECULIAR THINGS

PENGUIN BOOKS

PENGUIN BOOKS

Published by the Penguin Group
Penguin Books Ltd, 27 Wrights Lane, London W8 5TZ, England
Penguin Putnam Inc., 375 Hudson Street, New York, New York 10014, USA
Penguin Books Australia Ltd, Ringwood, Victoria, Australia
Penguin Books Canada Ltd, 10 Alcorn Avenue, Toronto, Ontario, Canada M4V 3B2
Penguin Books (NZ) Ltd, Private Bag 102902, NSMC, Auckland, New Zealand

Penguin Books Ltd, Registered Offices: Harmondsworth, Middlesex, England

First published in Penguin Books 1999
1 3 5 7 9 10 8 6 4 2

Set in 10.75/13 pt Monotype Garamond
Phototypeset by Intype London Ltd
Printed in England by Clays Ltd, St Ives plc

For Alice

Prologue

The morning I found him, he had been assembling a portfolio of his work.

'Portraits, mainly,' he said, leaning over the table to hide them from me.

'Any self-portraits?'

'A couple.'

'The true you, thank you Jeff Shue,' I said. He laughed. 'Can I see?'

'No.'

'Please, Jack?'

'*No*,' he insisted, covering them up. 'You'll see them when they're hung.'

I had my coat on. He was waiting for me to go out, but I sat down on the sofa instead and said that I was sick of it, finally sick of it.

He looked panicky. 'Sick of what?'

Ultimatums weren't my thing, but he sensed one coming, I think.

'Of not being allowed *in*. I can't stand it any more.'

He closed his eyes, shutting me out again.

'You can't do that to a child,' I said, 'even if you can do it to me. She has a right to know about her own father.'

'To know *what* about me? What does she need to know?'

I didn't bother answering.

'Nobody has a right to know anything,' he muttered, his eyes back on his work as if the crisis were through.

'You're such a hypocrite, Jack.'

'What about the right to silence, what do you think of that?'

'They're abolishing it.'

'Of course,' he said. 'They would.' But he exercised it while it was still allowed.

'Please,' I said. 'Please Jack. I love you so much.'

'Then leave it,' he begged. 'I've told you so much already. How much more do you need? Have you ever thought *why* I haven't told you more? For God's sake, I've told you more than most people would even *want* to know.'

'You've told me fuck all.'

'I was unhappy. Now I'm happy. What more do you want?'

'But you can't cordon me off from the unhappy part of you.'

'Well actually, I can. I do. And I always intend to.'

'Fuck you,' I said.

'If you don't like it, leave.' It came out of nowhere, a fist in the dark, winding me.

'What?'

'Then stop bloody going at me like some yappy dog,' he said, too fiercely. 'We're happy. You're pregnant. We've got a bright future. Leave the past where it fucking well belongs. Dead and buried.'

I could have hit him. He had won again, just like he always did. Because he knew in his heart of hearts that I agreed with him. It was the same thing I did of not wanting to know who my real parents were. How every time Mum and Dad offered to talk about it, I said, 'What's the point? It won't make us happier, any of us.' So I walked out and slammed the door. It was the last conversation we had.

I took the stairs when I came back, two hours later, weighed down with vitamins and health foods and more pregnancy books. I thought I needed the exercise. We lived on the fifth floor of a mansion block, which had a central staircase. Circular. I was doing that thing of counting the steps superstitiously, right foot first, hoping for even numbers at the top of each flight for luck. I was very superstitious in those days, as if I always knew that there was something wrong, something that needed more than human power to put it right.

I didn't see him until I was on the last flight, on step number seventy-three. I only paused at all because I was on my left foot when I should have been on my right. It was just his feet I saw at first, out of the corner of my eye. Even when I recognized the shoes, I thought it was somebody else, someone from the flats upstairs, because he was hanging from the wrong territory, from the landing above ours, so it couldn't be him. I even called to him through the door that there was somebody hanging out here and to come quickly.

I left the shopping outside our door and climbed the last flight, very unwillingly now, because as soon as I looked properly I could see that it was him, of course I could, straight away, even though the top floor was so dark. I could practically smell him, the way you can with people you love. I was going slowly, as if I might be better able to cope if I gave myself time. It looked as if he had killed himself, but I knew that he hadn't, that it wasn't what Jack would do. He was hanging from the banister by a thick belt. His mouth was open like it sometimes was when he slept, and his tongue was hanging out like a dog's.

I sat down on the top step. Next to him. I looked at him very hard for clues. His hair was over his eyes, but they were open, I could see that much, and they looked frightened. But I couldn't see what had happened, or how, or why. I kept looking at him, trying to see what it was, and then looking away again and blinking so that my tears would clear, so that I could see properly through them, and then I'd look back again, hoping to see something different, but he was still there.

I could hear Maria sweeping at the bottom of the stairs, right from the bottom flight, all the way up. I listened to the sound of the brush sweeping away the dirt as if I couldn't do anything else, until she was nearly on the last flight. She stopped. I looked down at her. She was staring at me with her mouth open. I had my mouth open too, I couldn't seem to close it. This strange noise was coming out of it so that I couldn't speak. She came and sat next to me and put her small plump Italian arms around me and let me cry on her.

She tried to get me back into our flat but I wouldn't move, so she took my keys instead and phoned the police and my parents, and made me some coffee, strong and black like Greek coffee with too much sugar in it. 'For energy.' I thought that my baby might die too, if I didn't do something positive very soon, so I drank it for her.

The police came first. They were kind and tactful, and Maria answered most of their questions. There seemed to be an unnecessary quantity of them milling about, up and down the stairs, in and out of our flat. Mum and Dad arrived soon after, puffing up the stairs. When they saw Jack they went white with shock. Mum was very good. She just looked at me, as if she understood. As if she could carry some of the grief herself, if I wanted her to. She didn't even join me at the top of the stairs. She waited for me to come to her, which I did fairly soon. And then a policeman asked if it would be OK for them to move the body now and I pushed him against the wall and started hitting him. 'He's my husband,' I said. 'We're having a baby.'

The policeman held on to my wrists so that I couldn't hit him any more, until Dad pulled me away. Lots of other people seemed to be staring at me. I didn't know who they were, but I shouted at them to stop fucking staring, and didn't they know that people died sometimes?

Mum guided me into the flat and locked everyone out and said, very calmly, that it was all right, that I was going to be OK, that I would feel very shocked and ripped open, but that I would come through it in one piece. I clung to every plain, sobering word that she said. But I didn't believe her.

Dad said that I ought to believe her, that she had been through more sorrow than I knew.

Somebody knocked at the door and asked if it was too soon for them to take the . . . to take my husband away? Mum looked at me and then went out and said something cross and came back. 'He's still there if you want to see him,' she said. 'I've asked them to give you some time.'

Dad looked nervous, as if she had done the wrong thing. But she had done the right thing, and when I opened the door, the place was empty.

I went upstairs to the landing, where he was lying on his back. His eyes were still open and his tongue was still hanging out. Next to him was a stretcher to carry him away, with some kind of zip-up bag on it. I pushed them aside and lay down with him, nuzzling against his chest. I tried to put his arm around me, but it kept falling down. I must have tried more than twenty times, as if it would make him alive somehow, and the moment at which I gave up was the moment at which I had to admit he was dead.

When I said, a few days later, that he wouldn't kill himself, Mum said, 'Well . . .'

And Dad said, 'He plainly would, Na, because he did.'

I said, 'That's what it looks like, I'm not denying that. That's what we're meant to think. But it's not what he would do.'

'Don't torture yourself,' said Mum.

I was close to screaming. All the time. At everyone. I had to keep getting away on my own, out into fresh air, or anywhere really, as long as it didn't have people there.

'We had a row that morning,' I admitted.

'There you are,' said Dad.

Mum shot him such a daggers look that he was lucky to survive.

The day Jack died was the first day of the seventh week of her life. She had just matured into a real foetus from a mere embryo, proper arm-buds reaching out for him. We'd bought our first book as soon as I had done the test. Every night we used to sit up and read it, studying the pictures, going over and over the different stages of her little life. Like excited children, we were.

It only feels like yesterday, all that.

'Sweetheart?' I had called out to him, full up to bursting with it.

'Hang on.'

He'd been in the dark-room at the time. The door was closed and the red light was on. I waited impatiently.

'Fuck it,' I heard him curse. 'Fucking under-exposed.'

I couldn't hang on any more. 'Are you coming out, or shall I come in?'

'I'm coming out,' he'd said. 'Hang on.'

He'd opened the door. The print in his hand was a shadowy mass that came to haunt me. My smile was contagious, spreading across his cross face.

'What, Na?'

'Guess.' Ear to ear now, a grin like a harvest moon.

'You're not!'

'I am.' I was holding the test in my hand.

'Let me see it.'

He'd taken it from me. Kissed it. Cried.

The night before he died, he stood behind me and caressed my belly and told me I was beautiful. Which I was. I was more beautiful than all women ever were, the great big mother of earth carrying the weight of worlds. But when he died I could hardly carry myself.

Love's such an insidious thing. You hardly know it's happening. It creeps up behind you while you're just doing chores. Living from day to day. Then suddenly it's everywhere, it's all you can see, the whole great fabric of your life woven like a web around you.

He loved me. We were happy. So *why*? It didn't make sense.

People said it wouldn't make sense, it never does, that when a person kills himself no one understands why. No one expects it. It comes from a hidden place, a part of them we never knew. They said I was doing exactly what everyone does when a person kills himself. Denying it.

I said, 'Please leave me alone. I'll work it out for myself. I know he wouldn't do it. I know.'

But apparently this was also typical behaviour with suicides, so they didn't leave me alone. Which was partly why I took Barkwood House, in the end. After much pressure from Drake to make a decision. The house was Jack's because he was the eldest son, and when he died, the house became mine. Because he left his heir inside me. His air.

It was a curse, that house. I can say that with impunity now, without fearing for my life. I should never have gone there. I took it without thinking. To escape everyone's cloying pity. To cut myself off.

But I also took it because I wanted to look for clues, hidden in his childhood home, and for that it was worth it. To find something that would tell me what I already knew in my heart.

His immediate past yielded no fruit. I must have gone over those last weeks of his life a thousand times or more. I couldn't stop myself. All roads led me there. It was like an obsession, a compulsion. And I went further back too. Right back to our first meeting, all the way through our five years together. What people had said about him.

Friends, ex-girlfriends, even employers. I kept trying to make sense of it, like a riddle; trying to understand why, trying to see what I'd missed. I thought that if he really *did* do it, then if I looked hard enough I'd be able to see why. But you can't find what isn't there.

There was no note or anything, which apparently isn't so typical. People who kill themselves usually write notes. They don't suffer in silence, or if they do, they don't take their suffering with them to the grave. They leave it for you to bear. The unbearable. They try to explain it to you.

I'd known Jack's family when I was a teenager. But how much do you ever really know about another family? We were neighbours for a time. One heady summer in Devon when my parents took a cottage there. We used to hang out together smoking cigarettes. Players No. 10. I was an only girl and they were three boys, and I tried to be one of them. To fit in. But they were just at that stage when boys see girls as girls. In a collective way. I must have been a late developer because I didn't like their appreciation of my small breast-buds. I didn't like the difference between me and the three of them. I wanted to be closer, to have what they all had, that brotherhood. I was sick of always being outside, the one on her own. I wished I was a boy.

Most of all, I wished I was Max. The middle brother. He was the happiest of them, the most playful and free, and I carried a torch for him. I can't help wondering sometimes, especially now, if it was my memory of Max that made me fall in love with Jack. All those years later. When we finally met up again.

Jack was the eldest, Max was in the middle and Neil

was the youngest. Neil never said very much. The other two bullied him but he never fought back. Jack talked a lot, mostly in a cross way. And Max just laughed, pushing his hair away from his open face (my abiding memory of him). He used to tease his brothers mercilessly, so that Jack got even crosser and Neil said even less. And then he would wink at me and my heart would stand still. As if it were waiting for him.

So it was a shock to see him again, after Jack had died. Like a displacement. And a shock not least because, the year after our summer together, he had run away from home and never come back and nobody seemed to know where he went. There had been a row apparently, although Jack never knew the facts. Max had just upped and left, and nobody saw him again. Jack always talked about him as if he were dead.

And it was confusing for me too, as well as shocking, because I loved Jack now, Jack was my husband, I was carrying his child, and yet here was Max, my original love, the seed, and Jack was dead. It was like a bad joke. Because, at the time, I felt that I needed someone so badly, in a way that I never had before. It was such a primitive feeling, as if being pregnant makes you want particular people as well as particular foods. A kind of craving. Maybe it's just the vulnerability, the thing of needing a protector, a guardian for your child. A man.

To begin with, it was Jack's lawyer, Nicholas Drake, to whom I turned. Not in a sexual way, I don't mean that. He was like a father, really. He provided everything that my own father did not, could not, in a crisis. He was immensely reassuring, and always seemed at pains to protect my best interests. *Chivalrous* is the word. The way men aren't, any more. Dad didn't like him. He never actually met him. He just didn't like him on principle. Because he wasn't Alfred.

'You should talk to Alfred about all this,' he'd insisted, after Jack's death. 'I've invited him to tea.'

'About all what?'

'This business of wills, what your options are. What you could do with that place, Barkwood. I did mention it to him. He seemed to think – '

'Dad! I'm a grown-up! I can deal with my own affairs.'

'Well you could do a lot worse than – '

'I don't *want* Alfred's advice.'

After a short pause, Mum set to work on me, reproachfully. 'Come on, love,' she said, laying out Alfred's favourite Battenberg cake. 'He's your father's oldest friend.'

'He's so bloody old he can't even get up the stairs to that cruddy little office of his. He's in his dotage, Mum.'

A wounded silence.

'The least you can do is listen to him,' Mum suggested. 'If he's willing to come all this way, just to give you his expertise.'

'If I want his expertise, I'll ask for it.'

I thought about his 'expertise'; how it had turned my parents into timid, cautious play-safers. How, with all the love in the world, I still felt suffocated by the risk-free zone they inhabited.

'He's never given me bad advice in forty-five years,' Dad said.

And so he came to tea. And once again I was subjected to the excruciating experience of eating and drinking with him. Poor Alfred. Short fat balding Alfred. How repulsive

I'd always found him as a child. The way he slurped his tea. The way the pink and yellow crumbs of the cake fell all over his cheap brown suits. The way, when finally replete, he would suck each finger clean with a noisy smack of the mouth.

'What you must do, quite simply,' he advised me, his mouth so full of cake it was extraordinary that he could speak at all, 'is ask to see the will. And then tell me what it says. I bet there's a clause in it that lets you off the hook.'

'Maybe I don't want to be let off the hook,' I said.

'Nobody has to take a house they don't want,' he bashed on.

'Who says I don't want it?' I insisted more forcefully. But he still wouldn't hear. It was Dad he was talking to, not me. It was Dad who didn't want the house, as far as he was concerned.

'Make sure this – what's his name? Mallard?'

'Drake,' I corrected him, very irritably.

The crumbs in his mouth blew out in a fountain of mirth as he laughed heartily at his own ludicrous mistake. What little cake remained was washed down with a last loud gulp of tea.

'Make sure he's not up to any tricks, any "ducking" and "diving",' he chuckled. 'It's your right to see the will, you know.'

In many ways I was already quite reconciled to taking the house, if only in the short term. I was even quite interested in the prospect. Certainly Alfred's visit did little to change my mind. The idea that Alfred Wooster might be able to see a clause where Nicholas Drake could not seemed so preposterous, so implausible, that I could barely entertain it as a possibility.

'I've come to see Nicholas,' I told the receptionist.

Drake's door flung open and he extended a welcoming arm. 'Come in, Anna. How nice to see you.' He shut the door behind us, his arm still resting on my shoulder. 'How *are* you?'

'Oh, you know . . . not bad.'

'Sit down.' He guided me on to a comfortable sofa at the other end of the room from his desk. 'Would you like a drink?'

I shook my head. I was so close to tears I couldn't speak. Every time anyone showed me kindness, I felt caught so unawares. As if I were wearing this great armour around me which some people just couldn't see. They only noticed the feeble creature inside.

'I'm so sorry about Jack,' he said. 'Just so sorry for you.'

I bent over the pain in me, afraid that it would all spill out if I didn't hold it in somehow.

'It's all right,' he said. 'Cry if you need to cry. I've got time.' Drake, who never had time. He sat opposite me and watched me sob, as if he were holding me through some kind of fit, strong as an anchored ship. When finally I sat up again, he held my gaze unflinchingly. It was as if he were accompanying me, travelling deep into the darkness with me, making it seem almost bearable. 'Are you ready to talk now?' he asked.

I nodded.

'So what did you want to see me about, Anna?'

'Um – just the will. The house. I know we've spoken

about it over the phone, but I just wondered if . . .' I petered out.

'If what?'

'Well just suppose if I didn't want it, or something . . .'

'Don't you?'

'Well I haven't entirely made up my mind, but – '

'I see.' He frowned, concerned.

'I mean, I may well want it. I just wonder what would happen if for some reason I changed my mind.'

He nodded. 'It must be very difficult for you to make any decisions, feeling as you do. And of course, in your condition . . .' He paused. 'You don't *have* to take the house, you're under no obligation, of course. But I must urge you, as your lawyer, that it would be in your very best interests to do so. Particularly now that you're expecting a child. With all due respect, what other prospects do either of you have?'

I took it. I was in early pregnancy, making plans, needing to build a new nest. It was only when I got there, months later and heavier by far, that I really regretted it. Even though I wanted to make some sense of Jack's senseless death, even though Barkwood seemed the only place to start, I regretted it.

I kept looking for the narrative in his life; the beginning, the middle, the end, as if the first two could make sense of the last. But all I could find were odd moments, snatches in time, that offered up blurred images of nothing in particular. A day on the east coast. A meal in a pub. Hitting balloons in the air, the Christmas before last. Buying a new lens. Life seemed unbearably random after his death, as if there were no relation between one thing and another, no cause and effect. Just chaotic life. And then, just its brutal end.

When finally I arrived there, I faced Barkwood House as one faces the enemy, looking for victory. I didn't know that there was no such thing as victory over the past, that what has been has been. But I soon found out. The past lives on in the air, for better or worse. And if it is for worse, as Jack's was, all you can do is keep trying to claw your way out as it keeps dragging you back. But it's like quicksand, an unhappy past. It will get you anyway.

I

'What do you mean, he's left the house to me?' Jack had demanded, as if it were an affront. 'He hated me.'

'Evidently not,' Drake had said.

'But what about Neil? I thought he was going to leave it to Neil?'

'He's left it to you, Jack. You *are* the eldest son.'

'Fuck that It's archaic! I know he lived in the Victorian age, *but.*'

Nicholas Drake coughed, glanced over at me, smiled sympathetically.

'Can I sell it?' asked Jack. 'Split the proceeds?'

'I'm afraid that's not what your father wanted, Jack.'

'Fuck what he wanted! The guy's fucking *dead*!'

Drake looked at his watch, allowing the noise of heavy aircraft to pass. 'If you don't want it, of course, you are quite at liberty to turn it down. It will then go to your younger brother.'

'Neil?'

'Not Neil, no. Maximillian.'

'Max? But he doesn't even live in this country! He could be dead, for all we know.'

'Indeed, if he also refuses the property, for whatever reason, then it goes to Neil.' Drake looked at me again, as if I were the one with whom he could best communicate. 'However, if you do decide to accept the property, it will bypass your brothers entirely, even after your death, and be left in trust to your eldest child. Which is, of course, a very appealing legacy, is it not?' He said this in a way that you couldn't refute, even if you wanted to, as if it were an absolute fact.

'But is there *no way* I can sell it, Nicholas?'

'Absolutely not. Even with a Deed of Variation.' He paused thoughtfully. 'I have to advise you to accept it, Jack. It's an outstanding property, whatever your personal memories may do to colour it. But of course, if – '

'What about the money?' interrupted Jack. 'What's he done with that?'

'He left his capital in what he called my "capable hands".'

'Neil gets it, surely? Or if Max *is* alive, then they split it.'

'I think it is most likely that the money will go to charity,' he said.

'Typical! As usual, divide and rule! It's like a bad joke, frankly, leaving me that house. His last fucking act of violence.'

'I'm sorry to rush you,' said Nicholas, 'but I do have another client arriving shortly.' A brief pause. 'Do let me know what you choose to do.'

'You call that a choice?' Jack stormed out of the comfortable, oak-panelled room.

I hovered behind. 'He's just upset,' I apologized.

'Of course,' he nodded kindly. 'I'm sure you will persuade him to see sense. For his children's sake, if not for his own.'

My hand was at my belly like a reflex. 'I'm sure I will.'

'Are you ever getting married, you two?' he asked, tidying his desk.

'I should think so, one of these days.'

'I'd see to it, if I were you,' he winked. 'Why not pop the question yourself? It *is* a leap-year.'

'Are you coming?' demanded Jack. He was stooping in the doorway, twitching impatiently, tall and gangly and cross. Anger was like an aura around him, glowing brightly always. It lent him a kind of charisma that pulled people to him, the way people gather round a fire.

I felt the small seed of deceit plant itself in me, without even knowing what it was. A tiny pulse of separateness, of separate interests to guard. We walked out of Drake's warm luxurious office into the cold January afternoon. A forbidding sky hung like a curtain over us, stealing the daylight too soon. Rain was freezing in sheets as it landed, as though our earth had a chill running through it now that nothing could thaw. Jack put his arm around me, around us, pulling us to him, his little family. We clung together along Holborn and down Kingsway towards the river, looking for a bus.

'My babies.'

'Three weeks today.'

'How do you know?' he grinned.

'Because I do. Because I dreamt it afterwards. I was wearing a wedding dress and it showed.'

'It's a cruel choice,' he said, not listening. 'So fucking sadistic.'

I didn't see it like that, but I was outside it, thinking not of his past but of our future, our child. Our pitiful struggle to make ends meet, every day, month, year. The fear of it. The increasingly brutal world outside. The instinct to hoard, even to cheat or steal to get by, to shore up a wall against the flood of poverty.

'How can I win?' he sighed. 'If I take it, I steal from Neil and Max. If I don't . . . Maybe I can make it pay somehow, share the proceeds.'

He was so decent. Such a luminous integrity glowed from him, it almost burned you if you touched it. Or perhaps I idealize him now.

'Marry me, Jack.'

'Oh God.' He raised his eyes to the heaven he couldn't see.

'Oh God what?'

'Yes OK,' he agreed wearily. 'I'll marry you.'

'Bastard. Forget it.'

'Mrs Stubbs.' He grinned from ear to ear and stopped me from walking and kissed me full on the mouth like we used to. Like we didn't bother doing any more with so much else on.

I couldn't stand to be in the flat after he died. That was the other thing that decided me. Every corner of it reminded me of what I had failed to see. I put it on the market within days of his funeral, against everyone's best advice, including Alfred's, again. Whatever Barkwood held in store, it had to be better than those memories. I took the first low offer I got. I had to wait another three months for contracts to be exchanged, then a further month for completion. So I was six months gone, at the supposedly blooming stage of my pregnancy, when I went down to Barkwood House.

'Dad? It's me.' I tried to sound firm. 'I'm just calling to say that I'm taking the house. I've decided. I've sold our flat.'

A dumbfounded silence.

'And I don't want you to – '

'You're a bloody idiot,' he said. I heard him repeat what I'd said to Mum.

She came bustling on to the line. 'But *why*, love? Why go so far away from us at such a – such a *difficult* time for you? This is when you need us most.'

I'd made up my mind. I wouldn't need anyone most. 'Why do you always ask why?' I said. 'Why do you always have to be given a stupid suburban explanation for every single move I make?'

'Well,' she stumbled, affronted. 'Because . . . because we *love* you, Na. We want you to be happy. Safe.'

'Don't be so stupid! How can I be happy now? Jack's *dead*, Mum.' I said it as if it were somehow her fault. 'You've got to let go of me. Both of you. I'm in early middle age, for God's sake.'

A necessary silence, or so I thought at the time. In fact it was a huge rift opening up between us, pulling us apart. I couldn't stop it; it seemed to be happening outside me, like something I couldn't control.

'Very well, love,' she said, in her smallest voice. 'We'll try. We'll do our best.'

2

Jack's old Renault 4 was packed up with the things I'd chosen to keep. His things mostly; few things of my own. Not much for a life or a love, but I couldn't see out of the rear windscreen.

I went back into the flat for the last time. I lay on the floor in our old bedroom where the bed used to be, on Jack's side. To feel him again. But the floor hurt me. I had to stand up to cry, bent over myself like somebody out of breath with a stitch cutting into one side.

I drove slowly. The sun was so bright it seemed to bleach the landscape white, a warm hazy blur of light, the way it feels when you're flying through high cloud, climbing into the sky. As if I were dying too. But when I turned down the drive of Barkwood House, the sun disappeared so completely I thought it had gone out. Behind thick cloud. It was just the avenue of trees, huge horse-chestnut trees like a tunnel over me, but it seemed as if the whole place were suddenly in shadow, as if the house that I remembered with such mixed feelings, but had always thought so beautiful and original, was suddenly looming over me like a great brooding beast. Instantly I felt uneasy, as if I shouldn't have come, as if even Alfred had been right. But I couldn't go back, not now; I had nowhere to go. I'd pushed my parents away as if they had been killing me, and now they were moving house themselves. They wouldn't even have a room for me in their new bungalow. I'd sold everything. The flat, the dark-room, the equipment. The only thing I'd kept was Jack's Leica.

I was too full of grief and guilt to go anywhere or do anything but lie in the bed I had made. And I owed it to our child. I would stay at least until I had found out why. Until I could hold something up and say: This is why your father died.

I turned my car around in the forecourt so that it was facing away from the house, towards the drive. Ready, when I was, to go. I turned off the engine. The silence was immediate, immense as a wave that suddenly drowns you, pushing at your ears. I could almost hear her beating heart. Double time to mine. I stroked her agitated feet as they pushed out through my flesh, trying to reassure us both.

The only place I felt inclined to go was the churchyard, where we used to smoke. The house didn't attract me at all. Its quirky originality had lost all its charm, as if it had only smiled prettily to hide its murderous heart. The pretence was over. And now it was waiting for me. I heaved myself out of my car into the late afternoon sun, astonished by how small everything seemed. Perception is such an emotional thing.

He came out of the church like a ghost. Almost at once, as if he were expecting me. Tall and gangly as Jack with that same thick curtain of hair pushed carelessly from his face. Startling as the bright sun. A cold sun though, given up for dead, buried all winter under concrete grey.

He stopped abruptly at the sight of me, as if mildly

disgusted by it, by the crude fact of me there. An intruder.
'I'm Max,' he said, as if he didn't know me.

I nodded, but my voice eluded me, filling up with grief. And then something shadowy rose to the surface of my memory, but I couldn't make it out. Something abstract. A dead thing, anyway, floating on its back.

'I'm the one who got away,' he said.

Which had never seemed true, for as long as I'd known it. And it didn't seem any truer then. He looked like the one who hadn't got away.

'We've met,' I explained.

'When?'

'That summer. Here.' He shook his head. 'Don't you remember? Years ago.'

He searched my face. 'Of course I remember,' he said. 'I didn't realize it was *you*. Drake said – '

'Drake? Have you seen Drake?'

'I spoke to him. From Italy. He said Anna – that Jack had married an Anna and . . . but . . . I had no idea you were the same – the same Anna as . . .' He was feet away and stayed there, studying me. 'You look very different.'

I wanted to look the same. I wanted my future to open out before me again. 'I'm sure I do. I'm six months pregnant and more than twice as old.' But I was still tall for my sex. I still had straw for hair. My eyes were still too big and my mouth was still too small. I still looked more like a boy than a woman, even with my belly out. Didn't he know me, really? 'You look exactly the same,' I said. 'As much like Jack as ever.'

He turned away from me, banning the likeness, finding something in the middle distance very absorbing. 'I didn't ever think of you as marrying anyone,' he said.

'No,' I admitted. 'Nor did I.'

'Least of all Jack,' he said. He still wouldn't look at me.

'No,' I said. 'I was never exactly family-minded, was I?'

He raised an unbelieving eyebrow, something I always wished I could do, but neither of mine would go anywhere without the other one. He was looking down at my huge belly.

'Yes, well . . . I am now,' I stumbled, losing my voice again. It kept drowning unexpectedly under sadness, sudden waves of it flooding through.

He just stared at me. No kindness. He was looking for something, evidence of something. As if he was suspicious of me.

'The traveller,' I recalled. 'Max-of-a-million miles, Jack calls you.'

He frowned.

'Called you,' I corrected myself.

'I wish I'd seen him again before . . .' He didn't mention death. They never do.

If only people would stop faltering in their speech, I thought, stop fumbling with grief as if it's a duty. Like half-hearted lovers clumsily undoing clothes. Apologies for love. Apologies where love should be. *Sorry* where sorrow should open out like a wound.

'You only had to get on a plane,' I said.

He nodded, bowing his head as if it weighed too much. 'I'm sorry.'

The way he looked, I almost believed he was. If only he could talk about Jack, animate him for me, tell me things I didn't know . . . 'Did you ever see him again? After you disappeared,' I asked.

He looked out at the middle distance again, like people

look out to sea. Now I realize that he was already at sea; that when he looked out, he was looking for dry land. 'I meant to come back sooner,' he said, shaking his head. 'I – it's just that I . . .' His body started to convulse. Like a fit. Spasms of movement.

'Are you OK?' I asked quickly.

'Y-y-y-yes.' He seemed to be trying to control himself.

'Are you sure?'

He seemed to be curling himself around some pain inside, a physical pain. He was bent double with it.

'Max?'

'It's – it's OK-K-K,' he said. 'I'm n-n-not – I'm not ill. I'm j-j-just – j-just so – ' A sound I can't describe flew out of his mouth, almost my equal in grief. Sorrow splashed everywhere.

I missed the moment at which I might have reached out. Touched him. Felt his loss too. Something in me resisted it.

'I didn't mean to – I'm terribly sorry,' he said. He was calm again. As though whatever had troubled him was out of his system now.

Then, without warning, he walked away. Leaving me numb. A brief outburst of sun that made the cold more cruel. He was so like Jack as he walked down the hill towards the lake. The same lazy loll to his gait, sparing of energy, using his weight to ease him forward, like heavy cargo at sea. Jack's air, I thought, but not Jack at all. Not even Max any more. No warmth left. No constant blazing hearth to keep me warm.

What did you expect? I asked myself. When he was far enough away, I let out my own sound.

It was only then that I admitted to myself what I was

doing there. It wasn't simply my private investigation into murder or suicide. I had come to grieve.

It was an astonishing house. A fairy-tale place that you could almost put your hand through and find wasn't there. It belonged in Italy somewhere, hidden by cypresses. Someone had picked it up and put it down again in the middle of Devon. Coats of white paint tried vainly to shed themselves like layers of old skin, so that the stone could breathe. The windows looked out like wary eyes over an insular view. A small lake. A field. A wood. Its own little church and graveyard. The eery silence of the dead. Young trees pushing out from beneath the headstones. Unfinished lives still grasping the day.

'Burn me!' Jack had insisted. 'If I die before you, burn me. I hate that fucking graveyard. Being buried there really would be hell.'

'Where shall I scatter you then?'

'Put me wherever you like.'

'*Scatter*,' I said. 'Not *put*.'

'Scatter, then. Wherever. I commit my soul unto your careful believing hands. Throw me at your heaven,' he said. 'Just in case it's there.'

She stretched inside me like a cat so that her still-forming hands pushed out on one side and her feet the other and then she got hiccups again. I jumped up and down to make them go away.

3

It was almost dark before I braved the house. I took what I needed from the car and left the rest where it was. So that I could leave quickly the next day. The front door was two doors really, closing together in the middle. I put the huge key in the lock but the door was already open, and in the gloomy dark hall with its cold stone floor was a note from Max. Wedged in the frame of the large mirror there.

Hope you don't mind if I kip here. Max.

I thought I did mind, which surprised me. Max, of all people to mind. But I could hardly object. It was more his house than it would ever be mine. I took the note down and crumpled it up. As if this would make him go away. I threw the tight little ball of paper on to the floor and watched it settle in the grout between two flagstones. And then I stood still in the hall, listening for him.

Not a sound. Just a throbbing silence, like a pulse. The house's pulse. I longed immediately for noise, urban noise, the very thing I had wanted to escape. Cars, police sirens, people shouting, trains.

I climbed the creaking wooden stairs in search of a bed, my heavy belly dragging me down. I kept turning on old Bakelite switches that didn't work. The dark was so dark, pouring in like ink, spilling through open windows, filling up rooms. I could hardly see. I wished I was asleep. I wished I could wake up in our old flat with Jack beside me, rubbing his grey eyes that sloped down like a dog's at the sides, kind and constant. I lay down finally, and listened to the silence. Listened to my thoughts. What it meant to be back there again. To see Max. To feel Jack's presence and absence at once. I was feeling nervous. Menaced by the thought of murder, not suicide. Of who had done it and why. Of what the motive had been. Of Max reappearing out of nowhere after all these years. Of whether anyone wanted to kill me too. No one would hurt a pregnant woman, I kept reassuring myself.

But if they would, I was an easy victim. Breathless, tearful, heavy and slow on my feet. I was running from despair as though it was a tide coming in, a whole ocean slopping at my heels.

I didn't sleep at all. I stared at the back of my eyelids where I kept Jack's grinning face. His spirit floated around me like a child's cloud, soft and cushioning and white, waiting for her birth.

Once the sun was up, lighting the dust and cobwebs of the room, the chalky sky-blue of the walls, I closed the shutters and slept through until noon.

I was woken by a sharp knocking. I threw on my blue cotton dress and unlocked the bedroom door. I was expecting Max.

'I'm Laura.'

'Who?'

'Your sister-in-law.'

She was dull-eyed but bright-lipped, the craters of her

uneven skin defined through her make-up, her bouncing hair swept back in a black velvet band.

'I didn't know Max was married,' I said.

'Not Max! Heavens! Max! Is Max even alive, does anybody know?'

'I think – '

'I'm married to Neil, not Max.' Smile. 'We wanted to ask you to lunch.'

It was a kind gesture. But I thought this place was mine now. Mine in which to hide. People seemed to be moving through it like traffic, in and out, as if it was theirs too.

'We're only a hundred yards down the road,' she said. 'Nicholas Drake told Neil you'd probably be coming this week.'

'How is Neil?' I asked fondly. 'Does he remember me?'

She looked puzzled. 'Ought he to?'

'Oh I shouldn't think so,' I said.

'Are you pregnant?' she asked suddenly, glaring down at my belly, frowning hard.

'Yes.'

She looked up at me. Hatred crossed her face like an eclipse, and then she was smiling again, all jolly lips and pearls. 'Congratulations.'

'Do excuse me, Laura. I've only just woken up. I didn't sleep very well.'

She put on a look of compassion the way you put on a hat. 'Poor old you.'

I didn't want pity, anybody's pity, least of all a stranger's. 'I'm fine.'

'Oh,' she said. 'Are you?' A touchy kind of shock in her voice.

I sensed it would have been there whatever I'd said. If I'd broken down in tears and said Help me, Neil's wife, I'm only half alive in here, she would still have said Oh. Are you?

'Yes,' I said. 'I am.'

'Lunch then?' she almost ordered me.

'I haven't even had breakfast yet, thanks.'

'You mustn't isolate,' she said.

'Well actually, I must.' I couldn't hide the edge in my voice. 'That's just what I must do. That's what I've come here to do.'

I could smell her sickly scent mix in with the rotten air of the house.

'Here,' she said, scribbling on a piece of paper that she pulled from her handbag, 'our address and phone number, if you need us for anything. I intend to keep an eye on you, Anna. Sorry about that.'

'You will be,' I muttered inaudibly, as she bounced along the dark hall, her court shoes clattering down the stairs.

'We'd better not have any more,' Jack had said, stroking my invisible bump.

'I want ten.'

'If we only have one, he won't have to be the eldest. Or in the middle. Or the favourite youngest one. Neil was always the favourite.'

It was just after our quiet wedding. We were walking back from the registry office with my best friend Josie and her awful husband Jeff.

'Why was he the favourite?'

'Oh Na,' he sighed. 'You can't resist it, can you?'

'Resist what?'

'My bloody family. You didn't marry them, you married me.'

'I'm only responding to a piece of information that *you* volunteered.'

'Now now,' said Jeff.

I didn't pursue it, for once. It was our wedding day, after all. 'Poor Neil,' was all I said. 'That must be a burden to bear.'

'If we'd pandered to them a little more, Max and me, if Max had stayed in the country and I'd kow-towed a bit more, they might've let him go.'

Jack was over-responsible to a fault. Arrogant, really, to believe that his own little life could change other people's.

But then, it changed mine.

I dropped by for tea instead.

'Oh. Hello,' he said. 'You must be Anna.' He stood in the doorway, staring at me as though I was some sort of apparition.

'And you must be Neil,' I said, still struggling to see the family likeness in him. 'You don't remember me, do you?'

He didn't answer. I wasn't even sure he had heard. He just said, 'Poor old Jack,' and puckered his mouth.

'Awful,' Laura nodded, looming up behind him.

He's dead, I thought. He's fine. It is us who must suffer the loss. 'I couldn't make it to lunch,' I said, 'So I thought – '

'Of course! Come in!' Laura ushered me through their cramped, cluttered hall into the kitchen. 'Sorry about the mess,' she said. 'The trouble with a small house like this is you just can't hide your junk.'

Neil was standing in the doorway of the kitchen now, still staring at me. I hated being stared at, especially then, so pregnant that my belly-button protruded through my dress. No one to find me beautiful any more.

'We're trying for a baby too,' he said.

Silence. Like a wall I couldn't hide behind. A completely irrational dread invaded me. I struggled for the appropriate response. 'That's nice,' I finally managed to say.

She smiled. A sickly, insincere smile. But how could I talk, with my insides and outsides at war?

'It would be fun, wouldn't it?' she smiled again.

I could think of other words to describe such a scenario, but I kept them to myself.

'Well now,' she said, 'we were wondering when you were due. September, isn't it?'

It wasn't the sort of thing you could lie about. I wasn't even sure why I wanted to. In hindsight it's obvious, of course. These irrational urges, whatever they are, ghosts or God or unborn souls, they watch over us, whispering their wisdom.

'Anna?' she demanded. Her face was in mine, urgent and frightened, needing something from me.

'Sorry, what?'

She laughed, pretending ease. 'That's hormones for you,' she said in a high voice to Neil, who never seemed to smile any more.

'So *is* it September?' said Neil behind me.

'Something like that,' I said, vaguely. They glanced at each other.

I felt their antipathy as if it were tangible; almost a

competitive thing, as if I were suddenly in a race that I hadn't agreed to run, that I didn't know had started, that I wasn't sure would ever end.

I followed them into the garden. Laura looked about her for something. 'Where's the table and chairs?'

Neil disappeared instantly, as if accustomed to hearing orders in mere questions. Laura put the tray of iced coffee and ice-cream and tall glasses on the parched grass of their lawn. 'Oh these men, these men,' she said.

I couldn't share her contempt, if that was what it was. Men had been good to me. 'I like men,' I said.

'Yes, but you were an only child, weren't you? Whereas I grew up with four brothers.'

And I had a father, I thought. But I wasn't going to argue. The sun was hot and my breath was too short.

'Don't get me wrong,' she said, trying to hide something with her voice. 'I love Neil. I do. It's just that – '

'One table,' said Neil, erecting it before us and disappearing again.

She picked up the tray and put it on the table. The ice-cream was melting. 'Weren't you adopted?' she asked.

'Who told you that?'

'Clarissa did, I think. You met her, didn't you? Their mother . . . Does that bother you?' she asked.

'What?' I said, all the indifference I could muster in one syllable.

'Being adopted?'

'Why should it?' I said.

'Oh I don't know. I think – well, rejection by your own parents, it seems such a cruel thing.'

'It's not necessarily rejection,' I said.

'What else is it? Love?' And then, as if her unkindness

had only just occurred to her, she said, 'Sorry, how tactless of me.'

'I don't have a problem with being adopted,' I lied.

'But you can't even ask your mother about giving birth!' she exclaimed, as if there was no greater tragedy. She paused thoughtfully. 'I always imagine adopted people must feel as if they don't belong. Anywhere.'

Jack. Come back to life.

'Three chairs,' said Neil, opening one out behind me. A collapsible wooden thing that looked too light for my weight. I perched on it nervously, waiting for it to break. For something to break.

'One for you,' he said to his wife, 'And one for me.'

'Oh dear,' she said. 'The ice-cream has melted!' She talked in exclamation marks, hiding her terror under a forced cheerfulness. A controlled hysteria. Too close to the edge. I couldn't bear to look at her, at the panic in her eyes. The make-up was sliding like milky coffee all over her porous face.

What am I doing here? I was already gasping for air. But there was nowhere else to go now. Why had I sold our flat so idiotically fast? I'd virtually given it away, like somebody trying to lose loss. Shake it off.

'Where are you having your care?' she asked.

'My care?'

'Your antenatal care?'

'Oh. My care.' I saw my summer drag out ahead like a long evening shadow, trapped in conversation with her. Caesareans. Pain relief. Cots. 'King's,' I said. 'At least, I *was* having it there.'

'What happens if you suddenly stop?' asked Neil. 'Do they come after you?'

'I wouldn't think so, would you? Not the NHS these days. Too expensive.'

'Or will you keep popping up there?' she asked.

What was it to them? 'Frankly,' I said, like Jack always did, *frankly*, 'I don't think I'll bother.'

She seemed delighted.

'I'm a trained midwife. I could do it for you myself.'

I tried to smile. Her face expected smiles. *Tell me I'm nice. Smile at me please. I said smile. Please.*

I vowed never to drop by for tea again, always to refuse their invitations, and to keep the front door locked. Which probably meant I would have to ask Max to leave. He must have let her in, that morning.

Escaping from tea had the same liberating relief as leaving home had done. Like getting a plastic bag off my head, at last. Before it killed me. The lane was a tunnel. A thick green hedge either side of me, obscuring all views. Inside the margins, cow-parsley grew amidst long grass, visited by butterflies. Everything seemed trapped.

Funny, I thought, how different Neil looked from either of them. Always did. I turned down the drive towards the house and the sun went in again. Neil had sandy hair, almost ginger, with freckly skin. And he was really quite small. A slight young man. Whereas Jack was famously tall, like Max, with the same open face. Clear and glowing. Like ivory.

Where was Max? No one had mentioned him at tea. I began to wonder if I'd really seen him, until I went inside and recalled the note that he had stuck there in the hall. I stood looking at the closed doors around me, wondering if I dared open any of them yet. I could hardly brave the smell, let alone the invading squalor of the place. The damp and rot and dust. I turned the handle of the door on my left – I suppose you would call it the drawing-room. The curtains were pulled shut across the windows of the two far walls. A small line of light broke through on to the floor. The furniture was covered by old white dust-sheets, looking like misshapen ghosts. I crossed the room to pull back a curtain and let in the low sun. The dust was thick as snow, layers of it, even across the floor, tracing the path of my timid, hesitant steps. Too much dust to settle in so short a time. The room must have sat undisturbed for years. There was something so grimly stagnant about it that even death seemed more vigorous. I tried to kick the dust over my footsteps as I left, closing the door firmly behind me. It wasn't what I remembered. I kept saying so. I kept trying to retrieve what I did recall, like a dog digging for a lost bone. A kind, healing place. Somewhere to belong. A home. But what I was forgetting was that Mum and Dad had been with me that happy summer. My home had been with them. I went upstairs and looked out at the enclosing view. It was like a live thing, holding me in. The light was slipping away again so fast. Was the sun cheating me? Fading too soon. Always too soon. Before, when it got dark, I used to be able to switch on the lights, pour myself a drink, and really feel cosy. Before Jack died. Even when he wasn't there. Even when he was just in the world somewhere, working late. But now the darkness threatened to swallow me up, like a black hole, a gaping hole of need that reached beyond all reckoning, meeting me everywhere I turned. Still no sign of Max. I went to bed. But again, I couldn't sleep. Not for the life of me now, after such a day. Unease in my very bones. I lay on my side, like a shelter around her, keeping guard.

At three-fifteen in the morning I heard a sound I couldn't identify. A small, woodpecking sound, like someone hammering pins. I sat up on the bed and listened hard. It stopped. And then it started again. What was it? It kept stopping and starting, like the rhythm of all human life. Inconstant, but sure. My adrenaline had begun to invigorate her blood, too, and she was soon up and about in my belly, resenting my stillness, prodding at me to play.

Then I heard footsteps, I could have sworn they were footsteps, walking comfortably up and down the hall at the bottom of the stairs. Max? Or a ghost? My heart was like a rhythmic tribal drumming in my ears. Deafening. I tried to find some strength, some inner resource buried beneath my fear, but all I could find was a cry, a soundless bellowing cry for Jack.

The footsteps stopped suddenly. They didn't walk away. They just came to an abrupt halt. Mid-journey. Going nowhere. I felt that I could almost see who it was. Like a dream. *Almost.* Not clearly. No features. Just the vague mass of him, waiting there in the hall, waiting for me to come down. Waiting for me. A dark shadow waiting for me.

I tried to think of something else. I tried to think so hard. I went through our list of names again, laying them out in front of me like a screen, a wall even, something he couldn't pass through. Girls' names first, and then if it was a boy, which I knew it wasn't even without the scan to tell me so, why then boy's names too . . . *Jack Jack Jack Jack Jack* . . . I kept going. Right up until dawn. Until birdsong like a concert, its rhythm too rich to steal. And then through dawn, more slowly now, sleep getting at me. I dozed off. I woke to find the sun crawling up through the shutters and over my belly, like someone caressing me.

It was nearly noon before I braved the hall downstairs. Nobody was there. Daylight makes fools of us. Noises in the night seem harmless at once, attributable to a hundred different things. I tried to wear a lighter heart, but I didn't wear it long.

I went out to the car to fetch the food I'd brought down. A loaf of bread, some jam, a tin of tuna, some tea and coffee, and a carton of long-life milk. Fairly unappetizing, but I'd eaten nothing except biscuits and ice-cream for two whole days. I was ravenous.

I ventured towards the kitchen for the first time, at the back of the house, away from the hall. It smelt. A rotten, sulphurous smell. Another blue room, it was. Pale blue walls with white-and-blue painted cupboards. Two large dressers crammed with crockery; mostly blue and white. A heavy wooden table in the middle of the room, stained here and there with cooking oil, rings where mugs had stood, marks where knives had chopped through bread, vegetables, fruit or flesh.

I struggled to open one of the large sash windows, but they were both stuck up with too much gloss paint. I stood on a kitchen chair and pushed furiously, scraping at the paint with an old loose nail, hitting at the wood. I had to pause for breath, my lungs so high and tight in my chest. As I balanced there, sucking in the clammy air, I thought I heard a creak behind me. Like someone standing on a loose floorboard, only much quieter, as if they were behind a door. I didn't dare to look round immediately.

Even if I'd had the courage, I couldn't seem to move my head. Fear was holding it still. It was as if I could feel someone there, and yet I knew I was alone. I didn't believe in ghosts, not even with all those noises in the night, so it didn't make sense to me at all.

I tried to think clearly, but my brain was a sluggish thing, refusing instruction. What it once processed in seconds, it now refused even to attempt. I stared at the window, wondering how best to break it. All I could think to do was to throw myself through. If it came to it. An escape route of sorts. One that would end in miscarriage, at best. But it gave me the courage I lacked.

I turned to confront him, every muscle in me ready for a fight. But nobody was there. And yet I didn't believe it, didn't believe my eyes as they settled on empty air. Somebody was there. Somebody had been there, irrefutably. I *knew* it. I could still feel their presence haunting the room.

Then I noticed that the kitchen door was closed. I'd left it open, very deliberately. The only doors I ever closed in that house were doors that I could lock. The front door, the bathroom and the bedroom door.

What now? What the fuck now? This time my brain was fast. Or faster. It suggested, as a weapon, the large china blue-and-white bowl sitting on the dresser. I thought of opening drawers, of finding knives or rolling-pins, but there wasn't time. I hauled the bowl down, a heavy great punch-bowl that needed both hands. I had to rest it on the table while I opened the door. I grabbed it again as soon as this was done and hovered in the doorway, clutching it over my enormous belly like a shield. Armour. For war. I was expecting violence.

Nothing. Nobody there.

I sloped along the dark corridor towards the hall, the weight of the bowl dragging me down. Once in the hall, I reached to undo the lock on the front door, but it was already open.

How? Unless Max was up.

'What on earth are you doing?' said a voice behind me.

I spun round to face him, my heart in my mouth.

He was standing on the staircase, about halfway down, wrapped in a blue towelling dressing-gown.

'Max.'

He waited for his answer, his eyes searching mine suspiciously.

'I was just – just – ' I didn't know whether to put the bowl down or break it over his head. He seemed so unlikely an aggressor. He looked as if he'd only just woken up. Scarcely conscious after a good night's sleep.

But as he moved towards me, his bare feet made no sound except where the wooden staircase creaked. I clung to my bowl, not sure that I even had the strength to lift it high enough for his head. I tried to, but he was already so close, reaching out towards me.

The sight of his hands outstretched, coming at me like strangling hands, paralysed me. A corpse already. Rigor mortis set in.

'Let me help you,' he said, prising the bowl from my grip.

Too late. It sat cupped in his hands like a papier-mâché hemisphere. Light as anything. An easy comparison of our respective strengths.

'Where do you want it?'

'Oh,' I said, surprised. I thought he knew exactly where I wanted it. 'Anywhere. I was just going to – just trying to cheer up the hall.'

He laughed dryly. 'You'll be lucky,' he said. 'It's innately sombre, this hall. This whole house, in fact.'

He put the bowl on the marble table beneath the mirror. 'Here OK?'

I nodded, smiling sheepishly. I had misjudged the signs. He wasn't going to kill me. Yet. 'I wasn't – taking it – stealing it – or anything.'

'It's yours to take anyway, isn't it?' he said.

'Is it?'

'House and contents, I think.'

I felt myself blushing. I remembered how Drake had said he would decide where the money went. 'How much did you get in the end?' I asked Max. 'You and Neil?'

'Get? What do you mean?'

'Of the money?'

'What money?' He frowned at me. 'We didn't get anything.'

'*Nothing*?'

He looked at me guardedly. 'You knew that, didn't you?' His head was cocked to one side as though listening for some remote sound.

A heartbeat perhaps. A racing pulse. A lie.

I blushed ridiculously. I always did, when people doubted me. 'Absolutely not,' I said. I only knew about the house.'

I felt shocked. Ashamed. As furious with Drake as Jack would have been. But I also felt more terrified than ever. What better motive for revenge? For creeping about in the night, plotting my 'suicide' or my 'accidental death'?

I was about to say, *Max, you have the house, you and Neil. House and contents. I don't want any of it.* But at that moment he turned away from me. Quite sharply. The way Jack used to when he didn't like someone.

'Have you had breakfast?' he asked, moving towards the kitchen.

'Er . . . I'm not – not really hungry. Madly.' Starving, in fact. But not at all keen to be back in that room. 'I think I'll just get some air. A bit of midday sun.'

'Midday already, is it?' He seemed to be feigning surprise. 'I must go to bed earlier and get up earlier,' he said, watching me for evidence of some feeling I didn't have. 'I can't seem to sleep,' he said, adding casually, 'By the way – did you see Neil yesterday?'

For some reason, I felt I'd done something wrong. 'For tea, yes. Just for a cup of tea.'

'Does he know I'm here?'

'He didn't say.'

'Do something for me,' he asked, but it was more like an order than asking a favour. 'Don't tell him.'

He sauntered off towards the kitchen. As soon as he was out of sight, I went outside. She was frantic inside me, like a bird trapped in a cage. I stroked her heel as it pushed against my restraining skin. My Wren. Jack had kept calling her Wren. I said it was a silly name, no one is called Wren, but now she was no one else.

The sun had been on my car all morning. It threatened to cook us alive. So I walked instead, out along the lane towards the nearest village, for food. The shop was shut for lunch. I decided to kill the time by looking for our old cottage. The one we rented that memorable summer. But it wasn't there any more. Someone had knocked it down.

4

I walked back from the shop slowly in the hot sun, clutching my small bag of groceries. Eating biscuits again. Letting her down. I stood at the top of the drive where the light vanishes and studied the house. It really was an unhappy place, I could admit that now. Not just recently unhappy like I was, in mourning for a love. Unhappy at the core, as if it always had been, as if it had never known joy. As if happy people had never lived there. How had I not noticed this, all those years ago? Or was it just that my own ordinary joy had been in the way, obscuring my view?

'Mother's dead,' he had said, putting down the telephone.

The tone of his voice, it was so dull, he might just as easily have been telling me the time.

'Oh Jack. No.'

'It doesn't matter,' he said.

'But she was your mother – ' I reproached him.

'She was never my fucking mother! She bore me, that was all.'

'But Jack, she – '

'She never *loved* us, Na. She never nurtured us, *mothered* us. She didn't have it in her.'

'But . . . they can't *both* have been so . . .'

'Can't they?' he asked, staring blankly at me. 'Can't you

conceive of people without love in their hearts? Open your eyes will you?'

Lovelessness seemed a heavier grief even than death. 'How did she die?'

'An accident,' he said. 'Apparently she fell down the stairs.'

I winced at the thought of it. Brittle old bones clattering down those stairs on to that cold stone floor. But there was so much more to wince about, that I didn't even know.

'"Jack,"' he said, doing his father's voice for me. '"Father?" "Yup. Me. Bad news, 'fraid. Your Mother's – er – dead."' The way he did it was funny, it always was, but I tried not to laugh. It didn't seem respectful to laugh.

'Poor old sod,' I said. 'He doesn't know how to feel.'

'He knows how to feel, Na,' he argued. 'He knows how to rage, doesn't he?'

And so do you, I thought. 'You ought to go down there,' I insisted. 'He needs you.'

'Like fuck he needs me. I needed him, once. Where was he?'

'Tit for tat is no way to live,' I said.

'Sometimes tit for tat is the only way to live. The only way to survive.'

'God, Jack,' I sighed crossly. 'What did he do that was so unforgivable?'

He turned away from me, protecting me from the cauldron inside him. 'If you want my children,' he said, 'don't ask.'

I bit my lip, and just as well I did. If I'd known even half of what had happened in that house, Wren wouldn't be here. And I would feel her absence every second of every long day.

We just went down for the funeral, in the end. Which was the only time I saw the place again, and then only fleetingly. We were ten minutes late. The mourners were huddled together in a tiny congregation, filling the first two pews of that cold little church. We stood at the back, Jack grinding his teeth furiously throughout. As soon as the coffin was carried past us and into the churchyard, he grabbed my arm and dragged me back to the car, tripping over her mound of freshly dug earth. He snatched a fistful as he went. Threw it into her grave. That was when he said the thing about burning him.

I walked up the dark drive again. It was like a recurring nightmare, that drive. I always seemed to be at the beginning of it, retracing old steps. Getting nowhere.

Max appeared to be waiting for me, standing outside the house with something in his hands which he held up to me. 'Fresh catch,' he said. His rod was propped up against my car.

'Where did you get those? Not from the – '

'Freshwater trout,' he nodded towards the lake. It didn't look very fresh to me. 'Will you join me for dinner?' he asked, like you ask someone out for a date.

Proper food at last. I owed it to her growing bones. 'Why not?' I agreed.

'Good.'

I was hot and tired from my walk. I went inside. Cleaned out an old cast-iron bath with some cleaning stuff I'd bought at the shop. Soaked in fresher water for a while.

When I came downstairs again, he'd made a sort of improvised barbecue out on the terrace.

'Very impressive,' I said. 'When did you learn to do that?'

'When I left here,' he replied. 'Survival skills.' He cooked. I watched.

He had laid the dining-room table so that it looked strangely grand, all things considered (the rising damp, the peeling paint, the dust). He'd chosen a table-cloth the colour of fire, musty smelling, creased where it had sat folded for years in some old cupboard somewhere. He'd used plain white china, which had a fine border of silver at the edges. Silver candlesticks and silver cutlery. A flamboyant spray of freshly picked flowers. Gladioli, lilies, a silvery leaf I didn't know. I was already hooked in, the bait lodged in my mouth as if it had grown there. All he had to do was pull in his line.

'So why did you leave home, Max?'

'If you mean this place,' he said, 'if you can call this place *home*, if anyone can describe the environment in which I grew up as remotely homely – '

'Wasn't it?'

He didn't reply.

'Was that why you left?'

He looked up from the sizzling flesh of the fish, his eyes boring into me. 'Jack didn't say?'

'I don't think he knew, did he?'

He frowned. 'He didn't know *how*, but he certainly knew *why*.' He looked back at his fish. 'I take it he didn't tell you very much,' he said.

'About what? About you, or . . .?'

'About anything.'

'He told me enough,' I argued defensively. I wasn't going to have Jack's estranged brother knowing more than I did about him. Jack was mine. He was my husband. He trusted me most of all. 'So why did you come back?' I asked, making him the focus again. 'What was suddenly attractive about home?'

'This isn't home,' he said. 'This has never been home.'

'About this country, then.'

'Nothing,' he said in the same tone, but more emphatically, as if I still hadn't understood. 'Absolutely fuck all. I hate this fucking country.'

'Then why did you – '

'I don't have a home or a country,' he said, impatiently. 'I don't really understand the concept, to be honest with you.'

I was reminded of Jack, but I didn't say so. I said, 'OK. Let me put it another way. Why did you suddenly choose to come back to England after all these years?'

He shrugged, as if it hadn't been much of a thing. 'Because she wrote. And that was unusual. I never usually heard from anyone. I wasn't sure she'd even kept my address. Although she knew my bank account, of course, she could've . . .' He stopped mid-sentence, as though he'd said too much, as though he'd let something vital slip out of his net.

He was boning the fish. 'Suddenly I got this letter from Mother saying that she needed me, that I was to come immediately, that something had happened.'

'And had it?'

'Oh yes.' He pulled away a perfect skeleton. 'It most certainly had.' He put the bones to one side, so that they went on cooking until they were ashes falling through the bars.

The smell of the freshly grilled food was heady, transcending time and place, too sweet for any dark truths to invade. I could have been in the Mediterranean or on a Goan beach, drinking woody cold wine, watching the slow tide come in. With someone who looked so like Jack I couldn't bear it.

'Enjoy,' he said, passing me a plateful of open pink flesh in perfect symmetry.

He climbed in through the window with his own plateful. His place was laid ridiculously far away from me, at the other end of a table that could easily seat sixteen. I thought it was a joke, a dig at pomposity. I couldn't believe he was actually going to sit there. But he did.

'Is this how your parents ate?'

'God, no. They didn't even know what a barbecue was.' He was so proud of his barbecue, of its improvised efficiency.

'I meant – '

'They never cooked a meal in their lives. They had staff for that.'

'I meant,' I repeated, guessing already, 'the seating. The distance. This austere kind of formality. Did they – '

'Is it?' he asked, surprised, almost shocked.

'Well . . .' I hesitated. 'It's not exactly intimate, is it?'

I tried to laugh about it, but his face was already twisted up with strain.

'You're right.' He sounded angry. 'Of course you are. It's quite absurd.' He moved his plate and cutlery a seat away from me. 'Old habits die hard,' he muttered, and paused. 'Is the fish OK?'

'Delicious.'

He smiled briefly, like a praised child, before the muscles pulled at his face again. 'They always sat like that. Always. I never thought to question it. Even after twenty years away from their appalling habits, I can't escape them.'

The one who got away, I thought dryly. Jack never sat so far away from me. Jack loved me.

He had his head in his hands.

'So you came back', I ventured, 'because something had happened?'

He glanced up from his plate. 'I'm sorry? What?'

'Your mother wrote, you said.'

'Yes.' He took some salad.

'Because something had happened,' I pushed.

'Yes,' he nodded, anticipating me. 'I absolutely can't tell you what, I'm afraid.'

'Because you don't know, or because – ?'

'Because it's a secret.' He looked at me again, challenging me to ask. 'Not my secret, it doesn't affect me, but it does affect someone else. Quite significantly. So.'

'So.' If you won't say, I won't ask, I thought.

'It wouldn't be fair on – them,' he insisted.

'It must've been quite a big secret to get you back to this country after twenty years.'

'It was a secret that only I knew. One that I used rather cunningly to my advantage, in order to get away. I suppose I should have told Jack too, shouldn't I? Can you forgive me? We never learnt to consider each other in that way, that's the sad thing. You must remember how we used to fight.'

He seemed to be looking for some evidence of forgiveness already, as if it should be an intrinsic part of me. As if Jack couldn't have married me if it hadn't been. 'Didn't he tell you anything, that brother of mine?' he asked.

'About what?'

'About – his childhood. His family.'

He glanced down at the baby in my belly. My hands covered her warily.

'It wasn't a happy childhood, I know that much.'

'So he did tell you?'

'Yes, he told me that. Even if he hadn't told me, it wasn't hard to see.'

He was beginning to irritate me, pressing for how much I knew or didn't know, as if there were points to score.

'In what way wasn't it hard to see?'

'Well, he bristled – like a cat with his hair on end – whenever I talked about any of you. He had no interest whatsoever in seeing any of you. He fumed every time he had any contact with George. It was pretty obvious that he didn't much like his family.'

'But why? Did he tell you why?'

'What are you trying to prove?' I asked. 'So what if he didn't want to explain the particulars to me?'

He held his hands up in the air. A gesture of surrender. 'I'm sorry,' he said. 'It's a raw subject, I know. I loved him too.' He left it at that. Picked at his trout.

'What should I know that I don't?' I asked.

He looked up at me, searching my face for the requisite strength. I don't know to this day if he thought he found it there. You can't, can you? Find what isn't there. 'He wasn't at all happy,' he said. 'When I knew him.'

'Well, yes, clearly,' I said. It was an unspecific and familiar truth, one that I had already stated. But sorrow exposed me again, began its short climb to my face, pricked at my eyes like pins.

'Truly unhappy. None of us were happy, though. It wasn't just Jack.'

I nodded dumbly, wanting more. More clues, things I didn't know, new things about him, as if he were alive to surprise me still, however painfully.

'But Jack was the oldest,' he said, 'and the oldest always gets the worst weather, if you follow me. Like the walls of a house, one wall is always more exposed. The oldest gets the full blast of the parental storms.'

He glared at me, such challenge in his eyes, as if he were testing me at something without warning me. 'There were a lot of storms,' he said. 'Never very much sun.'

I took this in. Hearing Max say so made it seem more of a fact than it ever seemed, coming from Jack. Whenever I'd tried to get Jack on the subject, he skirted over it. I used to implore him to tell me more about it, but he'd just reply that childhood was the unhappiest time of his life. Full stop. Sometimes, I'm ashamed to admit, I thought he was ungrateful.

'Do you think Jack would – do you think he had it in him to – ' I cursed the surfacing grief that tripped me up.

He waited for me patiently, but I still couldn't see any kindness in his face.

'Do you think he could have killed himself?' I managed, cleanly.

He looked surprised. 'Of course. Why not?'

'Because – ' I fumbled again for words. 'Because – I just don't think he would.'

His suspicion hunted for something in my expression. 'Why not?'

'I don't think he would,' I repeated. 'When you love someone, you know.'

'*Did* you love him?' he demanded coldly.

'How dare you?'

'I only – '

'How *dare* you?' I repeated.

'Please. I had to ask.'

My hands were on my belly as though it was a trophy, a gold cup announcing my love, a prize with two handles to hold above my head, engraved with love. 'How dare you doubt me? You don't even know me.'

'I'm sorry,' he said, nodding. 'I don't, you're right. I don't know much about love either. Women, love, any of that.'

I didn't care if he did or he didn't. I didn't want to care. Just because I used to love him once. Just because he looked like Jack. Brought him back to me. 'You're so like Jack, physically,' I said, 'it hurts me to look at you. Same eyes, clear grey like rain. The same broken nose, same skin. Even the same hair, only yours is longer. But your mouth is quite different. People always say that character is in the eyes, don't they? There is a certain light in some people's eyes, for sure. Not literally, of course. An energy, something that comes through in a photograph, like a sort of aura. Jack had that. But actually I always think the character is in the mouth. In photographs of people's faces, it's the lines around their mouths that tell me who they are, how to find them.' I looked hard at his mouth, trying to find differences that were barely there. 'Your mouth isn't at all like Jack's,' I insisted. 'It hardly has any lines. It's like a model's mouth, a preserved mouth that hasn't smiled or shouted or cried or done anything. It's hardly lived.'

I thought I was safe, then. I thought I had put a barrier up that could never come down, that would make further intimacy impossible between us. But then suddenly I saw all this pain arrive at the back of his eyes, at the back of his whole face somehow, all right there waiting to be expressed, as if his face were a mask, an uncomfortable too-tight mask that he couldn't ever take off. And I felt such tenderness for him, so much love, I didn't know what to do with it. I couldn't give it to Jack any more, and I couldn't throw it away, so I just denied it was there. I just put it away, out of sight somewhere inside.

'You're absolutely right,' he said. 'It hasn't lived.' He paused a while. 'Or loved.'

5

I moved bedrooms after dinner. I wanted a telephone by my bed in case of more noises. So that I could call the police in an emergency. Or an ambulance. Or both. I came across Max as I was clutching my sheets and pillows, padding from room to room. I opened the wrong door, and he was behind it.

'Hello there.' He looked up from a book. 'What's up?'

'I'm so sorry. I was looking for . . .' I didn't want to tell him about the telephone.

'Who?' he laughed.

Not you, I thought. Please don't imagine it.

'Actually,' I said, choosing the lesser evil, 'I was looking for a room with a telephone.'

He frowned at once, almost angry. 'Why do you want a telephone?'

'In case I go into labour,' I said.

'God.' A different frown worried his brow. 'Are you likely to? When is it – coming out?'

'Oh, not for a while,' I replied.

'How long is a while?'

'Several weeks,' I said, 'but you can't be sure. It might be early.'

'Several weeks early?' he asked.

'Oh yes. Babies are born very early sometimes.'

'I see,' he said. 'There's a room with a telephone at the end of the corridor. At least I think there is.'

'Thanks,' I said. 'Goodnight.'

He tried to smile.

I lay awake as usual. Too much food in my big belly, the heartburn getting to me. Something was getting to her too. She wouldn't lie still. And I was doing a lot of wondering. The kind of wondering that would keep anyone awake. About why Max had come back. About why he had stayed back when everyone else had died. About what he had been doing last night. That odd tapping noise. What was at the back of my mind, what was gradually making its way to the front of my mind, was a deep suspicion of him.

He wasn't at the funeral, was he? In spite of his mother's letter, he hadn't returned by then. Perhaps he only thought it worth his while to return after they had both died. Hoping for a legacy. He didn't look as if he had any money of his own. Where was it, if he did? He had no possessions of any kind, unless the fishing-rod was his. And when he discovered that nothing had been left to him, that it was all Jack's, he had killed him. He hadn't known about the baby.

Well, I was looking for a murderer, wasn't I? And he had a motive.

I was startled out of my thoughts at midnight by a terrible crashing sound. It came from downstairs. When I went out into the corridor to see what it might be, his bedroom door was open, but he wasn't in his bed.

The next morning, after no sleep, I picked up the

telephone receiver and fiddled with the old dial. An antique forties phone. Pretty as anything.

'Could I speak to Nicholas Drake?'

'Who's calling?'

'Anna. Anna Stubbs.'

'One moment – I'll see if he's free.'

Pause.

'Drake.' In a half-a-second-to-spare voice.

'Hello, Nicholas. It's – Anna.'

'Yes?'

He waited for me to explain the nature of my call, but I didn't know quite how to put it without sounding incredibly mean.

'How can I help?' he asked, trying to hurry me.

'I just – I wondered what my rights are, here.'

'Your "rights"?' he repeated.

'My rights. Where I stand, as regards Max and Neil.'

'I'm not at all sure I follow you.'

I didn't think he would. 'They seem to – well, to – be here.'

He paused. 'By "here",' he said, 'I take it you mean Barkwood House?'

'They seem to have keys, as well as Neil's wife, and – '

'Neil's wife?'

'Yes, and they – '

'Who is Neil's wife?' I got the impression he had the file in front of him again, and was thumbing his way through. 'Does Neil have a wife?'

'Laura.'

'Laura who?'

'I don't know. Laura Stubbs, I assume.'

A little exhalation of exasperation was just audible. 'When was he married?'

'I haven't the faintest idea.'

He paused. Cleared his throat. 'Go on.'

'Well it's just that they seem to come and go as if the place is still theirs. I mean, it's not theirs, is it?'

He didn't answer me.

'Is it? Or have I misunderstood some essential point about this whole transaction?'

'I think,' he began, cautiously, 'my best advice to you would be to tread very carefully.'

'Well of course, it's very – '

'It's a very delicate situation indeed.'

'I'm well aware – '

'Much more delicate than you could possibly know.'

He was beginning to irritate me.

'Are you still there?'

'Is there something I should know?' I asked. 'I have the feeling there's something I should know that nobody's telling me.'

'And if there is?' he asked rhetorically. 'If that is the case, Anna?'

I couldn't believe the change in him. I felt as if, having got the result he wanted from me, he had dispensed with all that time-consuming civility once and for all. I began to sense another, infinitely less chivalrous, dimension to him, one that enjoyed secrets, as if it wasn't the intellectual power of his profession that he relished, but something much more insidious. 'Well if that's the case,' I said, 'I intend to find out.'

'And how do you propose to do that?' he asked.

I could almost see the smile on his face. 'I'll think of something,' I said.

Silence.

'Very well. Do keep me informed.'

I didn't think I would.

'But it strikes me that if someone isn't telling you something, there is very little you can do about it. You can't extract secrets. They live in the air.'

'Thank you for that gem,' I said.

He let my sarcasm pass through the air by his ear. 'Most of the time,' he continued, 'lawyers prefer *not* to be told secrets. Secrets have to be honoured, you see, and that can be very compromising.'

I think he must have hung up. At any rate, the line went dead.

I picked up the receiver again to call Jack. Without thinking. To tell him how frightened I was, how I needed him, how confused I felt. And when I realized what I had done, I sobbed for quarter of an hour.

Downstairs in the hall on the cold stone floor, I found my first clue without even knowing it. The cause of the previous night's noise. The blue-and-white china punch-bowl lay like a broken egg, smashed into pieces. I felt as if someone was trying to tell me something. Or even if they weren't, they were letting something slip. Something fall. On to a cold stone floor.

I stooped to look at the pieces; tried to see if I could fit them together again. It seemed likely that I could, so I assembled them into a pile, to glue at some later date, relishing the childish symbolism.

'Oh dear !' Laura exclaimed, behind me. 'Whatever happened here?'

She had just walked in. No ringing or knocking, no apology for her uninvited invasion of my privacy. It seemed to be her right, almost her birthright, as if the place were her own.

'Hormones again?' Her voice was a high descant recorder, played badly. Unmelodiously. Outside the centre of herself.

'I didn't do it,' I said.

'Don't worry,' she smiled patiently. 'I'll clear it up.'

'Please don't. I'll – '

'What is most extraordinary,' she ploughed on, scooping up my pile, 'is that the punch-bowl is in the hall at all.'

'I put it here,' I said. 'Yesterday.'

'Oh,' she said crossly. 'Why?'

'I thought – '

'George would have thrown a fit, you know.'

'Really? Was he prone to fits?'

'And so will Neil if he finds out.'

I was bewildered. That so trivial a thing could have caused such offence. Laura walked away down the hall towards the kitchen, carrying the pieces. I followed meekly, ashamed like a scolded child of something I hadn't done.

She put the broken pieces into a black plastic bag. 'Don't worry,' she said. 'I won't tell on you.'

It hadn't occurred to me that she would, that there was anyone to tell, nor indeed anything very much to tell them about. 'Tell who?' I said.

'Neil of course,' she said. 'Obviously.'

She collected the dustpan and brush and strode off towards the hall again.

'I'm sorry, Laura,' I said, following her closely, 'but it isn't even his bowl, is it? Frankly, it's not even his house. I don't understand.'

She was already bending down by now, huffing and puffing, shovelling the remaining fragments into her dustpan, but she stood up to look at me. 'You don't, do you?' she said. 'You don't understand anything about this family.'

She could stare when she wanted to, really stare you out. It seemed that there was somebody very strong somewhere inside her, hiding behind frailty, as if frailty was a kind of armour.

'What don't I understand? What am I supposed to understand? Please tell me.'

She shook her head, as if it were unspeakable. 'I can only imagine that Jack was different,' she said, 'Or you wouldn't have to ask.'

'Different in what way?'

'I didn't know Max,' she said, 'but I shouldn't wonder if he didn't have the same make-up as the other two. As George and Neil.'

'But what make-up?' I asked. 'What do you mean?'

'The rage,' she said. 'The fury in them.'

I didn't tell her how accustomed I was to Jack's temper. I wanted him to be different somehow. The exception to the family, not the rule. 'I didn't know it was a family trait,' I said. 'Rage.'

'Goodness yes.' She looked at me gravely, as if I still hadn't grasped the half of it. 'George used to beat them, you know. All of them.'

'Yes I know.'

'Neil, Max, Jack, all of them. Even Clarissa, sometimes, all through their married life.'

I thought I knew that too, although no one had told me.

'How . . . sad.'

'Sad?'

'Don't you think?'

'Maybe she asked for it.'

I couldn't understand what she meant, although it is too clear now. 'How badly did he beat them, do you know?'

She shrugged. 'I expect they all deserved it in their way,' she said. 'Boys can be very troublesome.'

I couldn't tell if she was serious, or if she was just trying to make it bearable. I tried to remember the George I had met as a teenager. The tall, mild-mannered man whom I had liked so much, whom everyone liked. The judge. The man with right on his side. The man with the power to forgive.

She stood up again and smiled. 'Is it a boy or a girl, do you know?' she asked, laying her uninvited hand on my stomach.

I must have sensed something, even then. I remember removing her hand, politely but immediately, as if recognizing the enemy it was.

'I don't know for sure,' I said.

Do not touch her. Do not *dare.* Do not lay your devious little fingers on my heavenly babe.

'I quite want a girl,' I said. How could I want anyone else? Anyone but her, opening up like a flower into full and perfect bloom and smelling of sweet fresh air.

'Oh,' she said coldly, and then laughed. 'I would want a boy, or Neil would divorce me!'

Because almost every sentence of hers was an exclamation, it was hard to tell what was a joke and what wasn't. I got the feeling that this wasn't entirely a joke.

'I'm sure he'd be thrilled with a girl,' I said.

A shadow of trouble passed across her face. 'A girl would be better than nothing,' she said, 'but a poor consolation prize. He doesn't think much of women, Neil. But then, nor did George.'

I felt that I'd accidentally peeped into the wrong room and seen something brutal there, although it wasn't a visual image, at all. I couldn't describe it in physical terms. It was just a sense, like a bad atmosphere.

'Have you been married long, you and Neil?' I was curious. Drake had sounded so surprised to learn of Neil's wife, I thought that there might be something in it.

'How long is a piece of string?' she said.

It was a bizarre answer to a very direct question. If she'd said six months, I wouldn't have thought twice. I wouldn't have been suspicious of her at all. But 'a piece of string'?

'Very well,' I said, 'when did you actually tie the knot in your long piece of string?'

'Oh, the actual ceremony!' A blank expression wiped across her face, like a cloth across a blackboard. 'We just did a registry office thing. Very low-key.'

'When, Laura? That's all I'm asking you. When did you marry Neil?'

'The actual date, you mean?' She looked at me like a caught thief. 'It sounds awfully maudlin when I tell you, but apparently it's very common to – to . . . They say that people often – often do it, you know, make love, perhaps "procreate" would be a better way of putting it, around the time of funerals. I think probably marriage is the same.'

I was none the wiser. There had been three funerals in the last year. 'You didn't attend either of the funerals, did you?' she asked.

Whose was she forgetting?

'We were at Clarissa's,' I corrected her. 'We couldn't stay long.'

'Ah.'

'And I was at Jack's.'

'Of course you were,' she said too fast, afraid I might break down, cry all over her, repulsively human. 'I wasn't, of course. I didn't really know Jack. I was sorry not to be there, all the same. He was burnt – cremated, I mean – not buried, wasn't he?'

It was his she had forgotten. Of course.

'You can pay your respects to his ashes, if you like. They're in the bedroom upstairs.' I don't know what made me say it. I think perhaps that I was testing her. Watching for her response. Waiting for remorse to march across her face.

'No, thank you. I won't.'

'Was George buried?' I asked, equally matter-of-fact. 'Or was he burnt, too?'

'Oh, goodness.' She stared at me as if I'd said something quite shocking. 'Don't you know the circumstances of his death?'

'What circumstances?' I asked, mocking her term. 'Are there circumstances?'

'They think he – oh dear – the conclusion was that he – killed himself.' I could feel ice flood through my blood. 'How?'

'Goodness, how awkward. I'm so sorry. I thought everyone knew. I thought that's what made his – Jack's – death so doubly awful.'

'How did he die?' I asked coldly.

'Car. By car. He – um – he actually drove off a cliff. Down by the sea. But there was such a fire, nothing was left of him.' She shook her head so that the coiffured ends of her clean hair bounced gleamingly to and fro. 'Awful. Absolutely awful. They only knew it was him because of the car. Middle of the night, you see. Nobody saw it. So I'm afraid he *was* burnt, but not in the sense that you mean. The funeral was more of a memorial. They buried what they could find of him.'

Why don't I know this? I wondered. Why didn't Jack say?

I felt trapped in the midst of something profoundly sinister, like someone already up to the waist in quicksand before they realize it, clutching frantically at straws, hoping for stronger stuff. The branch of a tree, at least, something with roots.

'And you married Neil after this second funeral, did you? This so-called memorial?'

'No. After the first, after Clarissa's funeral. Not straight away, of course. Goodness, that would've been awful. So disrespectful. We waited a decent length of time, I hope.'

I couldn't believe that she still hadn't answered me. 'So when? What was the date?'

'Well actually it was just before George died. In December.'

6

I went straight back to my room and locked the door. I sat on the bed, eating the air in great mouthfuls, but it wouldn't go down to my lungs. It clung to my throat like a sticky thing blocking the way.

I couldn't get the images out of my mind, a whole series of them. A car flying through the sky, the crash, a livid fire with George trapped inside, still conscious, perhaps even changing his mind. No, not changing his mind at all. Really wanting to die. That must be what suicide is. *Wanting* death. Desiring it. Even embracing it.

That impulse he must have found somewhere inside him to die, what was it? Not Jack's impulse too, was it? Not the same urge as Jack's, like a family custom, passed down the male line.

Or was George murdered too?

It didn't bear thinking about, but I had to bear it, I had to think fast, if only my shrinking brain would work for me. Piece the facts together, never mind broken bowls. Tell her the truth about how her father died. I went downstairs again. I wanted to visit their graves. Look at them properly. Study them for clues.

Laura was still in the hall, sweeping.

'Please don't bother with that,' I said, embarrassed by her servility. 'Please, Laura. It's not your job to clean up after me.'

She made some kind of tutting noise and then said, 'Are you all right?'

'Yes, thank you.'

'I'm sorry I told you like that,' she said. 'It must've been such a shock.'

She went on sweeping. She wasn't easy to escape. She kept wanting to talk, to corner me and talk like you want to talk to a new friend, someone who delights you, who makes you laugh and love. Someone you can trust. And yet there was nothing warm or connecting in her conversation at all. It was as if there was a terrible conflict going on inside her, two goals at crossed purposes, which made intimacy impossible.

I was right, in retrospect. She was caught between two posts and didn't know which way to run.

'Well, if I can't stop you sweeping,' I said, 'then I'll leave you to it.'

I was tired. When she was asleep in me, she was like a dead weight to bear. And she was a boulder inside me today, my legs aching at every joint. 'I must sit down somewhere,' I explained, 'before my legs give out.'

'Of course you must,' she said, offering me a chair.

But I was hungry to be outside, away from the house. 'I'd sooner sit in the sun,' I said.

'You must do just as you please,' she agreed, not hearing my need at all, launching into her next paragraph with a deep intake of breath.

She's nervous, I realized. Of me? Of something. It's fear that makes her talk so.

She had come to do the cleaning, apparently. She'd been in the habit of helping out at Barkwood, she said, ever since she'd lived with Neil.

It was hard to see any evidence of this, but I didn't say so.

'They used to have staff in the old days,' she explained. 'A housekeeper, a cook and all sorts.'

Even I knew that. Jack used to spit about it, the loftiness of it.

'But they were all old, Anna,' she said, looking hard at me for understanding. My name gave me a fright, as if it shouldn't be there somehow, as if it wasn't safe in her hands. 'And old people have a habit of dying. And when they died, George and Clarissa couldn't get the new staff to obey them properly. So Neil did it all.'

She told me these insignificant details so urgently that I began to wonder what I was missing in them. What clues. What was behind them.

'Neil obeyed better then, did he?' I asked.

Trouble cast a shadow across her face. 'He was always very good to them,' she replied, defending him against something I didn't know I'd said. 'They treated him awfully badly, you know, in the end.'

He could have walked, I thought.

But he couldn't, could he? According to Jack, he was trapped. Like a parasite is glued to its prey.

'They were very lucky to have you both,' I conceded, hoping for closure at last.

She smiled gratefully. 'I like to think so. I'd like to think we could do the same for you.' Her servility shocked me. The creepy insincerity of it. 'It would be such a pleasure,' she added.

'Thank you Laura, but I do my own cleaning, as a rule.'

'Do you?' she asked, passing judgement with her raised eyebrows, as if I wasn't good enough for the place if I did my own cleaning.

Of course I could use at least eight pairs of hands every day in a place that size, but not their hands. And I wasn't staying, anyway. Cleaning that damp rancid house would be somebody else's lot, in time. Not mine. Max's, no doubt. Or if he didn't want it, then yes, they could clean it all they liked, Laura and Neil. Wash the whole place away. Like a dirty mark. I just opened the front door, quite rudely, and walked away from her, out into the hot day.

I headed for the churchyard. For the gravestones. I needed to identify the gnawing, growing suspicion in my heart, so that I could start putting words to it. Start giving it form. Not that those two gleaming slabs of carved marble would tell me anything new. But they just might confirm something old.

Max was there, with a spade. He'd pre-empted me, got there first, beaten me to the post. I sloped away, hoping he hadn't seen me, but he called out. 'Anna!'

The reluctance in my step was undisguisable, but he didn't seem to mind. I don't think he was especially used to thinking about anyone else. I felt her stir inside. Wake up. She was like my *alter ego* sometimes, telling me how I felt, what I needed to do. I surrendered to Max's invasion of my privacy, as I surrendered to all their invasions in the end, because I had no choice.

'Did you see the bowl in the hall?' I asked.

'Of course I did.' He sounded surprised. 'You put it there yesterday.'

'But it's broken, Didn't you hear the crash? In the middle of the night?'

'No,' he frowned. 'What crash?'

'I thought it might've been you,' I said simply. 'In fact I hoped it was.'

'No,' he said.

He didn't seem to know quite where to put the spade.

He hid it behind George's gravestone, as if I might find its presence improper amongst the dead. Irreverent, somehow. I didn't care, frankly. It wasn't Jack's grave. Jack would be buried in the air.

'I thought I'd – tidy things up a little here,' he explained improbably.

I looked down at the clumps of mud and grass. I couldn't see any real improvement, to be honest. I thought he had made rather a mess of things. I wondered if tidying up was really what he was doing there.

'Did you find a telephone, last night?' he asked.

'Yes, thank you. I did.'

'Good.' He paused. 'Look, I'm sorry for what I implied last night. About your love – or lack of it – for Jack. I couldn't sleep afterwards for shame.'

He looked at me very intensely, chasing my forgiveness. I sensed that he wanted something else from me too, something more that I didn't feel inclined to give. It was as if he were hoping that I could release him from himself, unlock his emotional paralysis somehow, as if I must have done the same for Jack.

'You needn't apologize,' I said, lightly.

I was trying just with my voice to imply the distance I wanted to keep, and yet there was such a pull all the same, drawing me in to him. His eyes did it. They brought me to Jack. Whenever I looked. Whenever they settled on me. 'But it wasn't fair – it was cruel and suspicious of me,' he said.

'Why not?' I shrugged. What I couldn't say was how much I suspected him. I just muttered, 'There's a great deal to suspect.'

His eyes bore holes in mine. 'There is, isn't there?'

He waited for me to say more. I didn't, I held back.

'Do you really believe Jack was murdered?' he asked, as if finally allowing the possibility.

The word startled me, even though I had used it in the same context myself. It sounded so brutal on somebody else's lips.

'I don't know,' I said.

'Who would want to kill him, do you think?'

I shrugged. 'I can think of several people. Can't you?'

'But who?' he implored, not because he couldn't think of them himself, surely; he just wanted them named, he wanted to hear them from me. 'Who and why?'

I kept my hand close. 'Why would he want to kill *himself*? That's the first question you should ask. He wasn't the type, was he?'

'I don't know,' said Max. 'I don't know what type he was when he died. I thought the verdict was suicide?'

'Oh so what?' I snapped. I had had the same conversation so many times already, with so many different people. I was sick of being told that I was wrong, over-imaginative, in denial of his death, of the meaning or the manner of it. 'It's not as if I suspect foul play because I want to,' I said. 'I wish he *had* killed himself. At least then he would have chosen to go. But he was having a baby. We'd only been married a month. We were happy, Max.' I kept saying so, as if to persuade myself. 'We were really happy.'

'It's OK,' he said. 'I know.' He came close to me,

resting a hand on my shoulder. 'I've had all the same misgivings myself about his death.'

The relief of his admission was immense. I sat down on the grass and buried my head in my hands. Grief on top of grief, layer upon layer of it rushed to the surface, as if Max's suspicions had made Jack's murder a fact. An absolute fact that no amount of strength could bear. But when I looked up at Max, his face was implacable, as if he could bear it all. The extraordinary convulsion of feeling that had riven him apart only days ago never returned. His face was expressionless, as if nobody was in there, nobody was experiencing his life. A lack of emotion that seemed so incongruous with his words. And yet his concern seemed utterly sincere. Something about him didn't add up.

'Tell me what his last movements were,' he asked me kindly. He was sitting down beside me on the grass. His presence felt so like Jack's, so urgent. A bright, restless flame.

'His last movements,' I repeated dumbly, seeing in my mind's eye only the final jerking spasms of a hanging man.

'What you were doing,' he said. 'What he was doing, everything he said, everything he did. Don't leave out anything just because you think it's irrelevant. I might see it differently. It might be the only clue we'll ever have.'

I felt wary, as if he were inviting me to sign a pact with him, as if he would steal all he could from me and call it friendship. But he was so seductive too, as if he were saying, so tenderly, so beguilingly, 'Here, Anna, take my hand. I'll save you from the lonely hollow within.' He smiled kindly, as if we were the friends we always used to be, always should have been – more than should have been, were born to be. 'Or go backwards, if you like,' he suggested gently, 'from finding him.'

My breath still leaves me when I go there. I didn't have the courage then. I dragged my reluctant memory past his hanging body as quickly as I could, back over those last hours and days, scanning them for things I might have missed. New clues. Proof.

The photograph, that was what I remembered. The one that he had over-exposed. The one that mattered so much to him he could hardly concentrate on the biggest thing to happen in our lives.

'We mustn't get our hopes up yet,' I had said.

Jack was holding the test in one hand, the photograph in the other. He was glancing between the two.

'Not for the first three months.'

He was nodding vaguely.

'Once we're past the first three months, we can relax. Tell whoever we like.'

He wasn't looking at the test any more at all, he was looking at the photograph.

'Things don't usually go wrong after . . .'

He had moved away from me towards the light, holding the print up close.

'Jack?'

He had his back to me, so that I could see the print in his hand. An obscure black shadow smudged across the paper like a ghost.

'What?'

'Are you listening or not?'

He spun round on his heels, remorse across his face like something luminous. 'I'm sorry. I'm so sorry, Na. Sorry sorry sorry.'

He put the print down and held the test across his palms like it was a precious gift to bear. Which it was. Like gold or frankincense or myrrh, but a hundred times more precious. Life itself.

'Look at that,' he said. 'Just look at that.'

'What's the photograph?'

I was bending over it, trying to make it out.

'Nothing important. This is what's important. This line.' He was tracing his finger along the soft blue line that told us there was life in me. 'Blue for a boy,' he said. 'Is it a boy, Na?'

I was laughing, shaking my head.

'No, seriously. Can you tell from the line? Would it be pink if – '

'Don't be ridiculous.'

He kissed it again, and then kissed me. 'I hope it's a girl,' he said. 'I was a boy and I hated it.'

He closed his eyes, and although this was something he often did, I could have sworn that this time he was praying. Only he never prayed. Whatever he was doing, it was like a sort of prayer. And then he said, 'My father's dead.'

I snatched her back. Pure instinct. My blue life-line. 'When?' I paused. 'How? I don't believe it.'

He nodded and then shook his head. 'Last week.'

'Why didn't you tell me before?'

He shrugged.

'How did he die?'

'Don't ask,' he said. 'You don't want to know.'

'I do want to know. I have a right to know.'

'Yap yap yap,' he barked. 'Anna's rights . . .'

'He's my father-in-law, Jack.'

He closed his eyes again. 'He's not your business,' he had insisted. His voice was cold and hard.

'If my own family isn't my business, what is?'

'They're not your own family!' he yelled. 'Don't ever call them "family" again!'

I left it at that. Back off, I thought. You are with child.

I didn't tell Max about the photograph. I didn't trust him enough. He didn't trust me yet either; it was obvious. I told him everything else, every small detail of Jack's last twenty-four hours, but the photograph happened much further back, weeks earlier, just after I had done the pregnancy test, so I told myself it didn't count.

'It's funny,' I said to him. 'When I first got together with Jack, I couldn't stop asking about you all, especially you, wanting to know what had become of you. But he wouldn't even utter your names. He told me about your row, about how you had disappeared, but even that much I had to prise out of him. It was like having a door repeatedly shut in my face. I stopped trying to open it in the end.'

Max chewed the end of a piece of fat grass.

'I wish I'd persevered, now. I wish I'd tortured it all out of him so that I could piece it together now. I can't help feeling there's something I ought to know, some missing link.'

'Mmm.'

'I keep wondering about George's death, too,' I volunteered.

He pounced on this. 'Wondering what?'

'Were you back in the country by then? When he died?'

'What are you trying to say?'

'Nothing,' I deflected. 'I was just wondering.'

Pause.

'I wasn't, no. I didn't make it back until I heard about Jack. I had no idea that my mother's cry for help had been so urgent. When I heard that she was dead, I – I didn't really want to come back for her funeral, for either funeral, hers or Father's,' he said.

'But you knew about the circumstances of George's death, didn't you?'

'What circumstances?' he asked.

'The suicide aspect of it?'

'Oh that, yes.' His face showed nothing. The more there was to feel, the less feeling he showed. 'Yes,' he said. 'I heard about that from Drake.'

'Suppose Jack *was* murdered. Who says George wasn't? Who says either of them were real suicides?'

He nodded, already there, as if he had been there for days, waiting for me as I dragged my slow feet behind.

'Do you think George would kill himself?'

He shrugged. 'He had plenty of reason to. Plenty on his conscience.'

'Such as?'

'Don't you know, honestly?'

'I'm beginning to find out,' I said. 'And what I don't know, I'm guessing at. He was a bully, wasn't he?'

'He was a fucking tyrant.'

'He used to beat you, didn't he?'

'Just a little,' he said. He pulled up another piece of grass and chewed its juicy green stem. 'Beatings, funnily enough, are the most bearable aspect of violence. They only hurt the corporeal, and children are physically very resilient. It's the other stuff that kills. The emotional stuff.'

'What emotional stuff?'

'The cruelty,' he said very plainly. 'The soul bruises very easily, I think. And heals very slowly, if at all.'

'Be specific, Max, please. I've told you all *I* know.'

'Look,' he said, 'it's over now, that time. I have to honour Jack's wish not to tell you, if I can. I did little enough for him while he was alive.'

I felt like a child feels, shut out of a room. 'He didn't like you very much, did he, Max? He didn't like any of his family much.'

'Jack? I didn't like him either. I doubt that it was really a question of not liking each other. We just shut down, all of us. It was the only way to survive. That was why I left home, in the end. You asked me why; that's why. For survival.'

Perhaps he *was* the one who got away. At least he was still alive.

'So if George didn't kill himself – '

'Then who did kill him?' he finished off. 'Who would even dare?'

'Who would kill them both, George *and* Jack?'

'And then there's Clarissa, of course. Had you thought that far?'

'But Clarissa fell down the stairs,' I contradicted. 'That was an accident.'

'Was it, really? On to a hard stone floor?'

I thought of the broken bowl, of how like a sign it had seemed. I had already admitted the possibility of her murder without knowing it.

'Anyone who wanted to kill her only had to push.'

'Yes, I suppose that's . . . true . . . but . . .'

His eyes were boring more holes into mine. 'I wondered if it might be you,' he said.

'Me?'

'You had a lot to gain.'

'Me?' I repeated. 'Are you mad?'

'Am I? You tell me.'

'You go too far, Max,' I said, very coldly. 'You keep going too far.'

'Possibly,' he agreed. 'Possibly I do.'

Was he trying to frame me? Or just to mislead me, put me off his scent, make me think he couldn't be the killer if he was so suspicious of me?

'I don't think it was you, as it happens. I'm fairly sure you're innocent.'

I glared at him.

He smiled. 'If indeed we're talking about murder at all.'

'Big *if*,' I said, trying to make out that I didn't suspect him.

'But if we are,' he continued, 'if they were murdered, and you're innocent, then who was the murderer and why?'

'You were,' I suggested boldly. 'For the house or the money. Or both.'

'*Touché*,' he laughed dryly. 'So. It was either Neil . . .' He paused dramatically. 'Or me.'

'Neil wouldn't kill them,' I replied too fast. 'He was totally dependent on them.'

'Precisely,' said Max.

'Precisely what?'

'He was totally dependent on them.'

'So?'

'So it must have been me.' He smiled his inimitable smile and then started laughing. My skin felt like it was peeling off. I couldn't tell if he was laughing at me or with me. Friend or foe.

7

The next morning, Max left for Italy. Did anyone else know that he had been in the country at all? Apart from me? Or was that his perfect alibi? I felt as if I were falling between two stools. He was either a murderer or he was my only friend. But he was neither. Both. Was he telling me, or was he laughing at me, trying to say, 'Anna, you're mad, of course they killed themselves, or I'm a murderer'? As if suicide wasn't hard enough to bear. But then I would remember the noises in the night. Clarissa falling down the stairs. The broken punch-bowl. Jack. The nature of George's death. And I would think of murder again.

His departure left me hollow. The need that I'd been denying in myself, really since Jack's death, resurfaced so urgently, I finally phoned home.

'Hello.'

'Na? . . . Is that you?'

'Hi.'

'Where are you?'

'Here, where do you think? I'm here.' Silence. 'I miss you.'

'Is everything all right? The baby and . . .'

'Come and stay. Please.' Pause. 'Will you?'

'Of course.'

They came. They did their best to indulge my conviction

that Jack was murdered. They had heard it all before. They were worried about me. About the state of my mind. Terribly worried. Every day of their stay, their eyes followed me anxiously, reproaching me for the weeks that had elapsed since they saw me last, as if the only thing that could possibly explain our estrangement was insanity.

They wouldn't go, once they were through the front door. Not until Max came back from Italy. They stayed for almost the whole of July, and even with all their fussing about me, even with the damage I'd done, even with the way they paraded their wounds in front of me every day, I was so glad of them. On their last day, standing by their packed car, they couldn't resist going through it all again, trying to make me see sense.

'Has it occurred to you that he might just have been unhappy?' Mum ventured. 'He didn't have such a good relationship with his family, did he? From what you've told us.'

'That's hardly a reason to kill yourself,' said Dad.

'He didn't kill himself,' I said. 'OK? I *know*.'

We all went quiet for a bit.

'Where's your nearest hospital, again?' asked Mum.

'I've already told you,' I snapped impatiently. 'It's in Exeter.'

'But Exeter's miles away,' said Dad.

I was as nervous as they were, but I didn't want it to show.

'I'll be fine,' I said.

'You will not be fine. You'll be on your hands and knees screaming for drugs,' said Mum. 'The minute you start contractions, Anna, however mild, call. D'you promise me? Pick up that telephone and call. We'll be straight down. Promise me?'

'I promise you.'

'Good,' she sighed.

I sighed too. 'Anyway, I'm not alone. Max is back,' I said. 'And Laura is a midwife.'

'You've already told me how well you get on with both of them,' Mum accused me. 'You think they're all murderers!'

'Sssh,' I whispered, intensely, glancing about me. 'Please be discreet. They could be anywhere, listening in.'

Mum and Dad glanced at each other nervously, as if this were yet another display of my insanity. As if I were so far gone, I wouldn't notice such a mute exchange between them.

Mum smiled her placatory smile. 'Well, anyway.' She looked to Dad for support. 'Whatever they are . . . It's us you need now. Family.'

'That's right,' Dad chipped in supportively.

Jack, I thought. *Jack is who I need now.* 'I promise I'll call.'

Mum smiled, sadly now, holding back her fear. 'We can't let go of you that much, love. You're all we've got.'

I gave her the biggest hug I could, my belly jammed between us like a football. Max was standing at an upstairs window, tapping goodbye.

The tapping noise. I suddenly remembered it. It hadn't stopped, despite Max being away, and yet they hadn't mentioned it. Had they even heard it? 'Do you still sleep with ear-plugs at night?' I asked them, above the engine's growl.

They both said 'What?' and squinted, as if to see the words more clearly. Maybe they're so deaf now they don't need ear-plugs any more, I thought. They waved as they rolled off along the drive. Mum was at the wheel. They say that women grow more masculine and men more feminine as time goes by, but if I think back to earlier years, she was always at the wheel. I felt a wrench of sadness as their car disappeared from view. And a rising feeling of panic too, as if they might not come back, as if they might suddenly die, like Jack did, if I wasn't with them.

Max had kept out of our way since his return, exchanging fleeting greetings with us all, but very little else. One polite and rather stiff lunch was as close as we all got before they left. But as soon as they were gone, he came out into the sun to join me. He arrived behind me, soundlessly. I virtually collided with him as I turned back towards the house.

'Sorry,' I said.

'My fault.' He took my bare arm as if to steady me. His touch was too intimate for me. I tried to pull away but he held on to me. 'I've missed you,' he said.

I tried to take back my arm but he wouldn't let go.

'Please, Max . . .'

'They love you, don't they?'

'Mum and Dad?'

'They really love you.'

'Of course.' I kept on forgetting, or not believing, that George and Clarissa didn't love him. Them.

'You don't know how lucky you are,' he said.

'They're not my real parents,' I justified, putting their love down. Making it less enviable. 'My real parents didn't even want me.'

Actually, I believed that they were forced by unhappy circumstance to surrender me, and still suffered the loss.

When you don't know the facts you can invent any number of things.

Max didn't have that luxury. He kept hold of my arm as if it would save him. And then he let it go. Dropped it like you throw a thing away. 'One of the most particular effects of real love,' he said, as if it were an obvious mathematical truth, 'is the innate attraction with which it endows the loved.'

He wasn't even looking at me. 'And of course,' he added, 'the opposite is also true. What is unloved becomes unlovable.'

I didn't know what to say. 'How was Italy? I never really asked.'

'Hot. Busy. Rushed.'

He wasn't exactly inviting.

'What were you doing there?'

'Tidying things up,' he said. 'Loose ends.'

'Were you working in Tuscany, then, when you lived there?' I asked. 'I don't even know what you do.'

'Does it matter what I do?'

I shrugged my shoulders as if it didn't, really. But I thought it probably did. 'I was just curious.'

'I've decided to stay here for a while,' he said. 'Maybe a year or so. Maybe for good. Who knows.'

Here? I thought. 'Where?'

'This country,' he spat. 'This wretched little isolated isle that thinks it's an empire still.'

'Why, if you hate it so much?'

'Because they're dead,' he said. 'Because they can't do any more harm.'

'But Jack's dead too!' I said, my voice suddenly too loud, too uncomprehending.

Threads of pain shot through his ivory face like coloured silk. 'I've been thinking about him such a lot,' he said, staring out at the middle-distance again. At the view they had shared as boys. The wood on the hill. The field of golden corn. The church.

'Ow.' Her feet pushed down from my bottom rib to my hip, like a knife from the inside out.

'I'm so sorry. You must sit down,' he said, taking my arm again. 'Do you want to sit outside, or – ?'

'I'll have a proper rest, I think. Lie down. Thanks. I get so tired.'

'Of course.' He wouldn't let go of my arm at all now, and it seemed churlish to pull away. He helped me indoors and up the stairs as though I was an invalid. Easy to push. He sat down on my bed beside me, holding my hand, the heat of his life too sticky for me. I wished he would go away, but he just sat on.

'Well,' I said. The way you do. *Well.* I managed to extract my hand at last.

'I can see how he might have done,' he said.

'Done what? Who?'

'Jack,' he said. 'I can see how suicide could have seemed like an option to him.'

I didn't want to know. 'I can't.' I said.

'But you don't know. There's so much you don't know.'

'Like what?' I asked.

'Oh, everything.'

'What? Everything what?'

'I'll tell you later, when you're – '

'Tell me now,' I interrupted.

'I thought you wanted to sleep?'

'I do.'

'Then sleep,' he said. And then he did the oddest thing. He started stroking my hair. 'It's very glossy, isn't it? Your hair.'

'Hormones,' I said uncomfortably. 'Pregnancy hormones. They make your hair shine.'

'Like a panther's,' he said.

I thought panthers had rather shorter, darker hair than mine. 'I'll go to sleep now then,' I said. 'If you don't mind, Max.'

'Of course,' he agreed, standing up. And then stroked my hair again. It was almost as though he didn't realize what he was doing. Like a child. He just reached out and touched, because it appealed to him. 'Is it always like this?'

'No. Like I just said,' I replied, quite sharply, 'it's the hormones.'

He took his hand away immediately, as if it were burnt. 'Sleep well,' he said.

He didn't even close the door.

8

I didn't sleep at all. I didn't even lie down. I locked the door as soon as Max had left and sat back on the edge of the bed. The edge of loneliness. I missed Mum and Dad already. Their clucking fuss which always wore me out, but which so reassured me too. They flooded me with love, so that sometimes I feared I would drown. Sometimes I felt as if I were on my hands and knees, stemming the flow. And then sometimes it just felt like glorious abundance. As if I were their prize thing in life. Their trophy to polish on Sunday afternoons.

Or was it just that they pitied me?

This rage thing, Laura was right about it. I could see it in Max now too. In Neil, without doubt. Different manifestations of it, but the same root for sure. Max was quietly but intensely furious, as though his fury lent him a lightness, a swiftness somehow. Neil was heavy, a smouldering lump of resentment like a volcano.

And Jack, well, he had been a furnace. Even if he never took it out on me, never scapegoated me or anyone else, it was always there. I don't know how he lived with it. Unless . . . was that what killed him? He flared up at the slightest kindling.

Kind, those of kin. To kindle, to bring forth young. To inflame, provoke, incite.

What had George inflamed in his young?

I must have sat on the edge of that hard mattress for almost two hours, puzzling over all of them, before Neil marched into the hall downstairs. He and Laura had been conspicuous by their absence while my parents were staying, but as soon as they had gone, they made their presence felt. 'Anna?'

My name made me jump, as if it shouldn't be there, as if I were supposed to keep it a secret somehow.

The voice was a man's voice, and it wasn't Max's, so it had to be Neil's. A simple process of deduction, much like a detective's.

I unlocked my bedroom door. I wanted to tell him that Max was still in the world, that he had come back, come home, and that he crept about the house like a ghost, getting up to things. I wanted an ally, just in case. 'Hello Neil.' I hung my head over the banister and smiled.

He looked up. He was scowling. 'Where's Max?'

I didn't know what to say, whose side to be on. I shrugged. 'I don't know where he is.' Which was half true. He might have been anywhere, in or out of the house. 'Because I've just spoken to Nicholas Drake,' he said, 'and according to him, Max is here.'

'Really?'

'Yes really. And considering it was you who told him, I wouldn't act so surprised.'

His tone was so very unpleasant, so totally lacking in civility, that I immediately became uncooperative. Besides, it was a habit of mine to side with the under-dog, and that was what Max seemed to be just then. 'Well, he *was* here,' I said, 'but he went back to Italy.'

'When?'

'When was he here, or when did he go?'

'I'm not amused by your antics with words,' he said.

'I'm not trying to amuse you,' I replied.

'When was he here?'

'When I first arrived,' I said.

'Five weeks ago.' He was very exact about that. 'Was he already here, or did he arrive, like some vulture, looking for pickings?'

'He didn't strike me as especially vulture-like,' I said.

'Could you answer the question please. It's very important.'

'He was already here,' I admitted, suddenly feeling that Neil was on his scent too, as suspicious as I was.

'And when did he go back?'

'Why is it so important?' I asked.

'When did he go back to Italy, please?'

'About three weeks ago.'

He thought about this for a while. 'Do you know why?'

'No. I'm afraid I don't.'

He scowled at me, and then looked down at the stone floor of the hall.

'Sorry about the – bowl,' I said, wondering why on earth I was apologizing.

He looked at me guardedly. 'What bowl?'

Had Laura been true to her word?

'Somebody broke the punch-bowl,' I explained. 'I hope it wasn't of any great sentimental value. I don't know how it happened. Perhaps it just wasn't very steady, wasn't well placed. I shouldn't have put it there.'

'It was only a fucking bowl,' he snapped, as if I'd accused him of breaking it himself. Had he?

'I feel so bad,' I said, 'that you and Max didn't get anything. In the will, I mean. If I can – '

'Who told you that?' he barked.

'Max.'

'Max,' he repeated. 'Funny, isn't it, how Max arrives back in the country at this precise moment in time?'

'I'm not sure that he is,' I said. 'Back in the country.'

And then of course Max waltzed in, carrying a large bunch of freshly picked flowers. He looked like someone in love, enjoying the good things of life, in the midst of other people's terrible tragedies. Our tragedies. Mine. He was happy with his lot. Happy.

We were happy, I thought. So *why*?

He didn't see me. He only saw Neil, or saw the dark air around Neil like thunderous cloud. Brooding. Ominous. He let the flowers drop down by his side, in just the same way that he had dropped my arm two hours earlier. As if throwing things away came easily to him.

Neil stayed where he was. Standing his ground. It was like watching two fighters in a ring. I wondered which one would strike first.

'I was going to – ' Max started to say, but Neil jumped on the words, almost trampled on them.

'How long have you been here?'

'Not very lo – '

'How long have you been skulking about here, looking for crumbs?'

'What?' asked Max, the shock obvious in his voice.

'I thought you were supposed to be dead.'

Max's eyebrow shot up in disbelief. 'Am I? Who told you that?'

Neil looked immediately contrite, as if he'd gone too far, as if he might be wrong after all, as if Max might be more decent than he had credited. 'Why have you come back then?' he asked.

'I can't tell you that. Not simply.'

'Tell me unsimply then.'

'Wait a minute,' Max said in a different tone, a calming tone. 'Can we go a little slower please?'

Neil nodded.

'Let's say hello for a start.'

'It just seems odd, that's all,' Neil explained.

'I think you're jumping to conclusions, Neil.'

Neil nodded again, glancing up at me. Max glanced too.

'Oh.'

'Hello.'

'You're up.'

'Yes.'

'I brought you some flowers.'

'Hang on,' said Neil, 'I thought you said he wasn't here? I thought you said you didn't know where he was?'

'I didn't,' I said, covering for him without knowing why.

'She didn't,' Max agreed. 'I've only just got here.'

'So what are the flowers for?'

'Girls like flowers, don't they?'

I was reminded of that summer again, of the way they all used to compete to please me. Me the girl. The unknown quantity.

'I wouldn't know,' Neil shrugged. 'I don't understand girls.'

Max put his arm on Neil's shoulder, brotherly and kind, seeing his own plight there, misinterpreting him.

'Laura's not much of a girl,' Neil explained, 'In that respect. In the way of flowers.'

'Laura?'

'My wife.'

Max took his arm away again. 'When were you married?'

'Oh a while ago now,' he replied vaguely.

'Congratulations. When?'

'Come and meet her,' he said.

'I'm amazed. How long have you been married for?'

'It's not a big deal,' Neil shrugged uneasily. 'She's nothing special.' He sounded as if he meant it, glancing up at me again.

'What a thing to say,' I couldn't help remarking.

'He's only trying to make me feel better,' laughed Max, in his old sweet open way. 'Poor brother Max and his bachelorhood.'

'Come and meet her now,' said Neil again.

'I will. I'd love to.'

'Good.'

Neil led the way. Max looked up at me, laying his flowers at my feet. He smiled a smile that might have meant anything. And then he disappeared.

9

I remembered something else, watching the two brothers walk away down the drive without Jack, three feet apart and slow. Another clue. Much further back than the photograph. Memory is so elusive. You have to sort of step sideways, into your body. Let your senses wake up dormant moments in your mind. Just one small thing you see or hear or smell can be a door through which you slip into the past. And suddenly it is vivid. You're in it, living and breathing it.

I was fourteen again, right back there, in the middle of myself. I could have been anybody, it felt so unfamiliar and intense. A stranger in my own skin. The passion in me.

I was standing at the other end of the drive, where it meets the road, where the sun waits to wrap its warm arms around you. At the exact point where Max was now, only I was coming towards the house, and he was going away. It was early, just past dawn, the sun scarcely up, a hazy flood of light through the mist, birds in full song, air so sweet, and nobody but me in the world.

I hadn't slept much, but I didn't feel tired at all. I was full up to bursting with life, I couldn't have enough, I wanted to be awake for every minute of it, feeling and laughing and hoping beyond hope.

I was in love with Max. So much in love, I thought.

Head over heels for the rest of my life. Never to look elsewhere. Always to adore him. Never to lose faith. He was for me and I was for him and God had said so. Well you don't know, do you, when you're only fourteen? You can't see how much you have invented about the person you think you love. How much you haven't asked, haven't been shown, haven't seen. You just want. You just have to have.

We hadn't even kissed. In fact it was only the previous evening that I had put a name to my intense passion for him, that I had called it love at all. I had slipped him a note, which he may not even have noticed, since I tucked it in the pocket of his jacket while his back was turned. It asked him to meet me at dawn, as if it were a dual and not abiding love that I had in mind. Which was how I came to be there so early, my heart anticipating too much joy. I had to tell him, I had to confess my love, without his two brothers listening in. I couldn't let such a chance go.

I hoped that as soon as he found the note, he would know immediately what I wanted to say to him. I hoped he would be up all night, like I was. I hoped that when we met at dawn, he would stop my mouth with a kiss. Then we would marry and have children and be happy ever after. The End.

I didn't even recognize the clue that I could see so clearly now. I had no context in which to fit it, no experience of the dark world from which it sprang. But now I could take out this moment as one takes out a file, to look at in a new light.

The house was all windows that looked out everywhere, as far as the eye could see. Nowhere to hide, except behind that high old wall which marked the boundary between the estate and the road. Like something protecting a huge diamond.

As soon as I saw those two figures walk towards me, I dived behind the wall. I hadn't been able to make out who they were, but I had no adequate reason to give anyone for standing there at five-thirty in the morning. Except Max. But if it was Max, he would have come alone. He would have sensed the intimate nature of the summons.

I was in amongst the high hollyhocks in one of the two big beds on either side of the gate as you turn towards the house, cream and blue and deep blood-red, reaching for the top of the wall, catching the last of the sun. I don't know how they didn't see me, but if they had, they wouldn't have said what they said, so they can't have done.

It was George and Clarissa. Clarissa had appeared to be a little way behind George as they had walked along the drive, as if chasing after him. I could hear her calling out to him.

'Please, George, dear,' she kept saying, as she approached the gate. I couldn't hear George at all, no steps, no words, no breath. But I could feel his presence as strongly as you can feel thunder in the air. Oppressive. Too close. And then he came into view, like a dark shadow looming over me.

'Please George, dear,' she said again, much louder.

I could see her now, too. She was almost out in the road in bare feet and too few clothes. She was wearing a thin summer nightdress, and her pale yellow-white hair was all wispy and lost. The shrewd hard look which she always wore wasn't anywhere in her face to be found. She looked frightened. Timid as a beaten child.

George was standing with his back to me, still as a block of stone. Square. He was fully dressed. He always dressed very well, even when he wasn't working. During that short summer holiday he was invariably to be seen in a well-cut light summer suit, or very occasionally in just a shirt and tie, but always in a tie. His hair was immaculately greased and combed, so that you could see the lines where the comb's teeth had been. He seemed, really, the height of respectability. Perhaps that was why I didn't entirely understand, at the time, what was being said and done. I was trying to fit a round peg into a square hole.

'You can't punish me for something I didn't do,' she pleaded weakly.

'I don't know who else did it, my dear,' he said dryly, 'if it wasn't you.'

'But it wasn't my fault, George. It wasn't my choice. I was forced. Against my will – '

'Ha!' It was an angry sound he made, more like a crow than a man.

'Can't you even believe that? Can't you forgive me for that?'

He turned away from her towards me, his face sour and cruel.

'Please, George dear. Have some sympathy for me, please, instead of blaming me always.'

'Sympathy!' he exclaimed, as if it were the very last thing in the world that she deserved. 'Your dishonesty is risible, Clarissa, it is so blatant.'

'My dishonesty! How can you say so? You think only of yourself!' she cried. 'You think only of your own tarnished pride, as if I were nothing more than damaged goods to you now. But I'm your wife, George. Show me some respect, for heaven's sake! Please? Some kindness, some honour, for once in your life! I put up with everything from you, everything and more, and this is how you thank me!'

'This isn't how I thank you,' he said. 'I'll show you how I thank you, my dear.'

He turned back towards her.

She said, 'Please, no. Not again. Please. It was so long ago.'

And then I heard a noise which I couldn't identify. I had no idea what it was, it just wasn't something I knew, but now I realize that it must have been the sound of his hand across her face, because she covered it with her own hands and cried. She didn't seem shocked or surprised. It was as if she had expected it, sooner or later. All she seemed was sad. Defeated.

It was the next bit that I never had any trouble remembering, although I'd forgotten the details of it long ago. As soon as I had outgrown my crush, it ceased to have any relevance in my life.

'I haven't even told you the most essential thing,' she said in half a voice.

'What essential thing?'

'If only I didn't have to.'

'What?' he bellowed.

She seemed to shrink at his noise. 'The fact that Max knows.'

'Max knows what? About this, you mean? This sordid little piece of your past?'

She nodded, flinching slightly.

'Did you tell him?'

'Of course not!'

'Then how did he find out?'

'I don't know. Truly I don't.'

The silence was like a boulder between them.

'But he says he'll use it against us,' she explained. 'He's already told someone, so there's nothing to be gained from trying to shut him up.'

'I'll shut him up,' George vowed.

'You won't. There's only one thing that will shut him up. Which is why I've had to tell you everything in the first place,' she explained. 'I don't hold the purse-strings, do I? So I can't pay him myself. But if you don't want a scandal, you'll have to pay him. Quite a lot of money.'

'Money?'

'And freedom,' she added. 'If they aren't the same thing.'

'How dare he threaten me with blackmail!' he boomed. 'How dare he!'

Before she could stop him, he strode away from her back towards the house in his smart clean clothes, an almost military march to his step.

As I said, I was a late developer, and I was still at the end of my childhood, in a way. I hadn't yet turned that corner from believing that parents were usually right and children usually wrong, to realizing the unlikelihood of this. So although I couldn't follow the intricacies of what was being revealed, I thought that George, big good respectable George, was cross because Max had done something really wrong, and it did sound a little wrong to me, and it rather coloured my rosy view of him. Which was chiefly what I remembered of the whole conversation.

My own emotional journey from being deeply in love to being not so enamoured after all. The details went out of my mind. And even when I met Jack, years later, it was Jack that interested me, not Max. Not what Max had done or not done as a teenager.

Perhaps I didn't want to know. Just as I didn't want to know that Jack might have killed himself. And as I didn't really want to know that George had hit Clarissa then. Of course it was obvious that he had, but at the time I convinced myself that the red mark on her face was just emotion, or just the mark that her own hands had made. And when I saw her later on that day, she was all made up so that it didn't show, and I just forgot about it. I was only interested in whether or not I still loved Max. I thought I probably did, but probably ought not to.

10

An uncomfortable degree of feeling came back with that memory. Jack was dead and my old passion for Max was suddenly alive again. And she was inside me waiting to learn about love. What would I say? The great big immensity of it. I felt indecent somehow, as if I should wash myself or go to confession or pray.

I wanted to tell Max about the incident straight away, not about the love, but about the conversation between Clarissa and George. Ask him what he thought it meant. I had a pretty shrewd idea, or I thought I did, but I didn't guess the real nub of it at all.

I tried to be patient, waiting for him to return from his meeting with Laura, but I was like a schoolgirl again. Building up silly dreams about a better future than I had envisaged for months. As if I could turn my unhappiness around, make a loss a gain. Make Max the true love of my life, the whole magnanimous reason for Jack's suicide, as if Jack had obliged us, had always known, had lovingly stepped out of our way. Denial is a river in Egypt.

I estimated that Max's visit would not take very long, but I was wrong. He still wasn't back by the time it got dark. I began to worry. A growing feeling of panic began to surface in me. The feeling that he might never come back, that I would lose him too, that I was fated to lose all love, all men, all dreams. Fated to grieve. I walked down the drive towards the lane and stood looking in the direction of Neil's cottage, waiting for a tall figure to emerge out of the darkness. I couldn't face being alone in that house another night, with bowls being smashed on the floor, footsteps pacing up and down, strange tapping sounds. But the figure that eventually walked towards me was a small and urgent one, no easy loll to his gait. Somebody much busier than Max. It was Neil.

I felt instantly nervous, and found myself backing away to that same hiding place again. Although there was much more shrubbery to conceal me now, and it was nearly dark, I felt infinitely more visible to him. As if he could smell me, or hear my breath, as if he hardly needed eyes at all. Like an animal really, and I suppose that was what it was. He had an animal's instinct. While George and Clarissa had stood feet away from me for some minutes in broad daylight without seeing me, it wasn't actually me that they were looking for. There was no reason for them to sense me there. Whereas I knew that Neil was looking for me.

As he passed me he stood stock-still, as if he had walked through my aura, as if he could hear every dying cell of my life. I stopped breathing. I didn't even blink. I was suspended in time, like a freeze-frame. And then he walked on. Up the dark drive towards the house, the inky night blotting him out. Absorbing him.

When I couldn't see him any more, I set off down the lane towards his cottage, courage like a drawing-pin in my hand, too small by far but there. Just enough of it to make a difference.

I was losing my bearings in the dark, so I didn't recognise the place from the outside, but the lights were on inside and I spotted the back of Laura's head. I moved closer to the window, but not so close that she would see me. She was bending over something. I couldn't see what. Then she stood up and walked towards me.

I thought she had seen me, I thought she was coming for me, but she had only sensed me. It was the curtains she was coming for, the curtains she wanted to close. As she approached, she filled up the window with her form, obscuring the scene behind her, so that I couldn't see anything but her. Her face was matter-of-fact, as though she was just washing up or hoovering. But I knew she wasn't. I knew she had Max in there, and I knew that she was doing something to him.

She paused for a fraction of a second at the window, as if she could sense me too, just as Neil had done. Then she swiped the cloth of the curtains across the frame and I couldn't see anything.

I looked about me for somewhere to hide. Neil would be back soon, having failed to find me, having seen my car, plain as day, going nowhere. He would be suspicious and anxious and hurry back to tell her, and they would both wonder where I was. They would soon conclude that I was nearby, because where else would I go? And they would come out to look for me with torches and outside lights.

I didn't have very much time. I had to make allowances for the handicap of pregnancy. I couldn't run anywhere very fast if I had to, whereas Neil undoubtedly could. I backed away from the cottage, virtually into the hedgerow. It was dense and very unwilling to accommodate my large form, but I had to stay there because Neil was already back, I could hear him running towards me along the lane. He went straight past me this time, sensing nothing, and thumped at his own front door, which Laura opened. He stormed in and slammed the door behind him.

He soon opened it again. It seemed that I was right about the torches, but it wasn't necessarily me they were looking for, just anyone. Any sneaking witness to their deeds. The beam flashed everywhere at first, and then it came round a second time, more slowly, like a search-light. I don't know how they didn't see me. It shone straight in my face, and then it moved quickly on, over the remainder of the hedge. If they did see me, they let me be. For the moment.

They went inside again but returned in no time, hunched over something heavy, awkward to carry, even between two. It was a body. They were dragging a body outside into the darkness, wrapped up in a sheet. Neil was at the helm. He looked as if he had the body under its armpits, while Laura had its feet. She wasn't strong enough. She kept dropping it on the ground, and when she did, it made no sound, no life-like cry of pain. It was heavy and limp and very probably dead. And if it was Max then I loved him again more than the whole wide world and wanted him back. Because he was innocent and Jack's brother and so like Jack that it hurt.

'Careful!' barked Neil.

'I'm trying,' she replied, a little sharply herself.

They were stumbling towards an old Land-Rover that sat in the parking bay just a little way from the road.

'Put him down,' he ordered impatiently. 'Unlock the back of the car.'

She virtually dropped him in mid-air, as if Neil's orders

were making her much jumpier than carrying a dead body was. She came very close to me as she passed me by the hedge. I could have reached out and touched her, tripped her up.

She unlocked the back doors of the car, and then returned to help Neil, who was trying to drag the body on his own. She picked up the feet again.

It was all happening too fast. From months of speculation to this sudden, undeniable fact of the two of them guilty as sin itself. I didn't know what to do, how to stop them, whether I should. Whether I could save Max now, or whether I would simply be risking my life and Wren's for nobody else's.

I was already too late, it seemed. He looked so dead, it was astonishing. Absolute death shouldn't be possible in so short a time. It was the same feeling I'd had about Jack, that full, vigorous life shouldn't be allowed to just disappear without other people being consulted. Or at least warned, at least prepared for it in some inadequate way.

The back of the Land-Rover was open and Neil was already inside, frantically trying to drag his brother on to the floor there. Laura was fumbling hopelessly at Max's feet still, pushing at his legs, when really what she needed to do was to lift up his hips. I was almost tempted to help her, as though it wasn't a body at all, just something awkward to lift that needed another pair of hands. It was horrible to watch. It took so long.

Laura shut the door and handed the keys back to Neil, who walked round to the front of the car and opened the door on the driver's side. Laura climbed into the passenger's seat and then they were away, as if they were just off for the weekend somewhere, the car lights beaming up the lane.

I climbed out of the hedge and tried to open the cottage door but it was locked. None of the windows were open. I doubted that I could fit through any of them anyway, although I was tempted to break one and see. Instead, I chose to follow the lane back to Barkwood and telephone for help from there.

It was a clear, sticky night, the sky thick with stars, like scattered sugar over black treacle. What had they done to him? What did they do to Jack before he died? I felt very panicky. Too big for the speed necessary to outwit them. And I couldn't breathe properly. The oxygen, if there was any, wouldn't go down to my lungs. She wriggled inside me so forcefully. She seemed to be trying to get out, as if she wanted to run, as if she could sense the danger ahead.

I turned down the drive. Again. I was always there somehow, always at that point of no return. It was like a wrong turning you keep going over in your mind, thinking to yourself: if only I hadn't turned down there, if only I could stop now, have the choice again, things might have been so different.

Even at night the light seemed to disappear, or the ink-black dark spilt in, I'm not sure which. I could hardly see. The house was just a great shadow ahead, amorphous and menacing, until I was at the front door with my key in the lock, and then it was a solid place again. The door was already open. I couldn't remember whether I had locked it or not. For a fleeting silly second, I thought that perhaps Max was back, in the same way that I went on believing Jack would walk into my life again one day and put his big arms around me.

I crept up to my room in the dark. Very quietly. I wasn't convinced that I was alone, despite all evidence to the contrary. I closed the bedroom door behind me and turned the lock. I could hardly see in front of me. I tripped over what I supposed was my bed, but it seemed to be in a different place. And then I wasn't at all sure that it was my bed, I thought it was something else, something human perhaps, but I didn't dare switch on the light in case they were outside the house somewhere, still looking for me. If only I'd left the shutters open, I thought.

I was trying to find the telephone. The only number I could surely dial blind was 999, if I could find the bloody thing. Please. I bent down to feel my bed, so that I could follow it to its head where I knew the telephone was, but my hand came against something very like flesh instead. I let out a short scream. There was hair too. I seemed to have a whole handful of it, a thick mop of it, like Max's hair. I wanted to scream properly but my voice went somewhere else. I had the feeling that things weren't going to be all right, that I wasn't going to survive, that no help would come.

It was about then that someone grabbed me. Whoever it was couldn't see much himself because it was more like an embrace at first, until he realized which way I was facing. He turned me round so that his arm came across me from behind, his hand almost gripping my tender breast. His other hand came over my mouth, smelling of something unpleasant. Chloroform, I think. I tried to push it away. I was surprised by my own strength, when it came down to it. Life or death. Him or us.

'Turn on the fucking light,' he said. 'She won't keep still.'

I heard a movement somewhere near the door. So they were both here, in it together, the odds stacked up against me. But I wouldn't give up, wouldn't lie down, wouldn't surrender. It's such a primitive thing, the instinct to protect your young. Immense and deep and irresistible.

I tried to bite his hand. I got a mouthful of cloth at first, but then I felt the gristle of his knuckle and forced my teeth hard together.

'Fucking bitch!' he cursed, pulling his hand away for a brief second. 'Get that fucking light, will you, woman?'

'I can't find it,' she pleaded, the hysteria rising in her voice.

And then suddenly we could all see everything in the bare light of that naked bulb. Like creatures in headlights, momentarily stunned. Max on the floor bent over in a heap of sheet, looking very dead, although I couldn't see any blood. Laura by the door. Neil behind me. He loosened his grip on me for a fraction of a second and I slipped out of his hold. Then or never. I pushed Laura away from the door. She tried to stop me, but I pushed her a second time so that she fell. Neil was about to grab me again but I managed somehow to unlock and open the door and run.

I ran as fast as I could, which wasn't fast at all, almost falling down the stairs and out into the night. I couldn't use the weight of her to my advantage at all. I needed a miracle. He ran after me, and she ran after him, and there was nowhere to hide because he was at my heels and I couldn't get the distance.

We were only a few yards up the drive when I felt a terrible searing pain in my womb, like a saw cutting me in half. I collapsed at his feet, or he may have brought me down at that moment, I don't know. All I remember is the pain at the top of my womb. I was screaming with it, as if someone had cut me open there, a great rip of open flesh, right in the middle of me.

I thought I was dying. I thought he had killed me. He was standing over me, looking at me in astonishment, as if he hadn't meant to do it quite so soon. Laura came up behind him, looking at him and then at me, as if she thought so too. As if that wasn't the plan.

'I didn't touch her,' he said.

She knelt down at my side. 'Where does it hurt?'

I put my hand where it hurt and moaned.

'I think it's an abruption,' she said over her shoulder to him. 'We must get her to hospital.'

He said, 'Why hospital?'

'Because otherwise it'll die.'

'I thought you were a midwife!' he barked.

'Please!' I screamed. *Please save her.*

'I am a midwife.'

'So why can't you deal with this?'

'Because I'm not God,' she said, sharply, 'I don't give life. And I'd sooner not take it away.'

He laughed at this. At least I think it was a laugh. A coarse, cruel sound. 'If you don't get the car,' she said firmly, 'I'll have to call an ambulance.'

'But what about – him?' He gestured towards the house.

'What about him?'

'We can't just leave him there.'

'Why not?' she said. 'Best place for him. He's not going anywhere. And if somebody finds him, it's Anna's room they find him in. Anna's house, no less.'

Neil stood still for a moment, looking at us both. Then he kicked Laura, like an angry child kicks the thing that lets him down. He stormed off along the drive to get the Land-Rover. It was tucked inside the barn where I hadn't seen it. I could see the lights flood through the cracks in the wood as if it were on fire.

'It'll be all right,' she said to me. 'The baby. It'll live.'

I was the body now, lumbered into the back of the car like a second corpse. The pain was getting worse by the minute. I thought that in fact I would rather be dead if the pain didn't stop soon. And even if it did. I would rather be dead now.

11

I was losing a lot of blood as I bounced about in the back of the car. The floor was covered in it. Unless some of it belonged to Max. A mixture of his blood and mine. Some of it was definitely mine, I knew that for sure because every time we hit a pot-hole in the road, I could feel it pour out of me. I kept thinking – or hoping – that I was just wetting myself, but it was the wrong colour for that. Black in the dark.

The pain was getting worse, aggravated by fear of losing her. I don't know if I passed out. I think I may have done, because I don't remember anything about getting out of the back of the car and into the hospital. I only remember throwing up and moaning. A deep low sound, like a Buddhist chant, which made the pain almost bearable. A wave to ride. A wave to drown in. And then suddenly I was on a trolley, racing along a corridor and into a brightly lit room. Men and women were scurrying about in blue tunic tops and trousers like pyjamas, with bathcaps over their heads.

'One, two, three, LIFT,' someone said, and they lifted me over to another trolley, where they covered me in blue sheets and stuck needles into my arms, and strapped something cold on to my belly, which was hurting so much. A nurse or midwife or whatever she was said, 'She's with us again, Mike.'

And Mike said, 'Hello. I'm Mike Taylor. You've had an abruption – the placenta has come away from the uterus. It's a severe separation in this case, which means that baby is distressed and in danger.'

I immediately identified the sound of her heartbeat beside me on the monitor. Too fast by far.

'Please be quick,' I said.

'We're going to have to perform a Caesarean section, OK?'

'As soon as you can. Please.'

He nodded. 'We don't have your notes. How many weeks pregnant are you?'

'Oh, God.' I couldn't think. 'Thirty-six? Something like that.'

'And any problems during pregnancy? Any abnormalities?'

'No.'

'Have you had anything to eat or drink in the last six hours?'

'No.'

'OK. We're going to have to give you a general anaesthetic, I'm afraid. There's no time for an epidural.'

He had a needle already in his hand that someone had passed to him. I had blood flowing into one arm, and a clear fluid into the other, saline or something, and a catheter inserted into my bladder. I couldn't see where another needle could go, but he found a space and swabbed it clean and stuck his anaesthetic in. And soon I was hearing everything through a thick fog, a muffled incoherence of noise that made no sense to me. I wanted to tell them about Laura and Neil, about Max in my bedroom wrapped up in a sheet, but I couldn't get hold of the words. I had no control, I was being pulled away into a deep silence without any choice.

I wasn't unconscious for long, or so they told me. Forty minutes or so. But they were the most important minutes of my life. They took an eternity. And when they were over and still she wasn't in my arms, against my skin, at my breast, I thought she must have died.

'Where is she?' I cried to nobody. I couldn't see anyone, I seemed to be entirely alone in a room I didn't recognize.

'She's fine,' said a familiar voice.

I couldn't tell where the voice came from. Something heavy inside me was dragging me back into unconsciousness, stealing me away from her again. I had to fight it the way you fight defeat, every cell in your body concentrating hard on the goal.

'Where is she then?' I managed to ask.

'She's fine,' repeated the voice I still couldn't place. 'She's in Special Care.'

'Why? What's wrong with her?'

I began to wake up. I even located the direction of the voice and saw Laura there, sitting by the window in a saintly aura of light. 'What have you done to her?'

'I haven't done anything,' she said, 'except make sure she didn't get confused with anyone else.'

'Let me see her,' I almost shouted. 'I must see her.'

I hauled myself up in the bed, out of my cloying lethargy as it tried to pull me back. 'I must go to her,' I said. I tried to get out of bed, but there was an uncomfortable pull on my belly that surprised me.

'You've got quite a wound there,' said Laura indifferently. 'You ought to be careful.'

She didn't offer to help me. She turned away from me and stared out of the window at the sky. I eased myself out, my feet hardly reaching the floor.

Laura glanced at me, and I noticed the expression on her face for the first time. I wasn't sure how to read it. I couldn't tell whether it was hatred or pain, or even whether it was kindness. I didn't know her well enough. Thinking back to her expression now, I would say it was pity that she was feeling. Pity for me, for what was to come.

'Where do I go?' I pleaded. 'Which way is Special Care?'

She didn't answer. She didn't even look at me.

There was a tight feeling of panic in the pit of my stomach. A feeling that between the two of them, Laura and Neil, they might do anything to her, they might already have done it, she might already be dead. I opened the door into the corridor and asked the first nurse I could see to show me my baby immediately. I was beginning to feel the same shock of grief that I felt when I found Jack. The feeling that it couldn't be true, that if I just did something sensible very quickly, everything would be all right. She was kind, the nurse. Helpful and warm. She gave me her arm for support and took me into the Special Care Unit where the incubators stood, where all the babies were lying on their tiny stomachs under infra-red lights, trying to stay alive.

The nurse asked me what my name was and repeated it to another woman there. This woman was also kind. She led me to a tiny little yellow shape whose ribs pushed out through her too-thin skin, trying to draw in the air.

'Here she is, love. You can touch her if you like.'

I don't know why, but I felt so sad.

'Put your hands through the holes,' she said.

Perhaps it was her helplessness.

'Like this.'

Or perhaps it was just that she was all right after all.

She demonstrated the holes for me. 'They need your touch,' she said.

I nodded. I couldn't speak.

'She's on a monitor, that's what that is, and the tube in her arm is a drip. And that one is for food, and that's a ventilator.'

The nurse smiled. I looked at her because I still couldn't speak, but I wanted her to know that I appreciated her help. I tried to smile but all the emotion was pulling my mouth the wrong way.

She said, 'I know she looks very small and frail, love.'

She looks like Jack, I thought.

'But she's doing fine.'

A small frail version of Jack.

'She really is doing fine. She's going to be just fine.'

And then she understood that we wanted privacy, so she left us alone.

'Ask, if you need anything,' were her parting words.

I need to hold her, I thought. I need to take her out of her plastic box and put her to my breast. Feed her, cuddle her, let her smell my skin. I need to mother her.

But I just watched her, instead. I sat down and watched her for a while. My hands were shaking and I didn't want to touch her until I could keep still. She was fast asleep and only a foot long with soft hair like down stroking her tiny limbs. A short irregular breath went in and out of her lungs as if she were struggling for it, but her face looked so peaceful that she couldn't be struggling for anything. She seemed to think that she was still snug in the womb, warm and cosy and safe.

I put my hands through those strange rubber holes just to feel the air around her. It was warm as anything. Her own private sun. My hands were almost steady again but even so I hardly dared touch her. They looked too big beside her, too heavy for her. I ran a light finger along her tiny spine and felt her perfect vertebrae.

She stirred in her sleep and her mouth suckled the air. I had to take my hands away again immediately because of the feeling in me, the overwhelming tenderness of feeling, like a need I couldn't satisfy, to hold her in my arms too tightly for her tiny frame to withstand.

And then she opened her eyes. An astonishing blue, like sky, like the day breaking at last. They looked straight into me. I pressed my face against the box to be clearer to her.

'Hello, little one. Little bird.'

She blinked patiently.

'Aren't you so – perfect.'

Her eyes shifted a little over my face, and then she tried to suck her thumb but she couldn't seem to get it into her mouth. Her face creased up into a great big cry, all mouth, a screaming cry for me.

I ran to the woman who had brought me there and explained that she was crying, as if no baby had ever cried before, as if it meant that she was going to die unless I could hold her.

'I'm afraid you can't hold her yet,' she said, as she followed me back to my little hungry bird. 'But you can help feed her.'

'When can I hold her?'

'Soon enough,' she said reassuringly. 'Soon enough.'

By the time we were back at her side she was fast asleep again, her thumb securely lodged in her mouth.

'There we are,' she smiled. 'She's fine. She won't be getting very hungry, love. Her stomach is very small.'

I put my hands in the holes again and stroked her tiny back and the perfect shape of her head with its fine etching of hair.

'Will you be feeding her yourself?'

'Yes, of course.'

She smiled approvingly. 'Would you like to express some now? Ready for her next feed?'

'Oh, yes please. If I can.'

So she passed me over to a nurse who took me to a breast-pumping machine and I was milked like a cow.

I sat beside her all night and most of the following day. In case anyone tried to steal her from me. I fell asleep in the chair until someone suggested that I might prefer a bed. I was shown into a room where three other mothers tried to comfort three big babies, while mine lay, tiny and alone, in a plastic box. I was much too far away from her, but I was so tired I couldn't even argue.

I slept in fits and starts. Every cry beckoned me. I kept going to check on her, to make sure that she didn't need me, before I could sleep again. Oh Jack, I kept thinking. Jack Jack Jack. If you could see her now.

I found a few coins to call Mum and Dad, as I had promised to do *before* she was born, but I couldn't remember the telephone number at their new bungalow. I couldn't even remember their address. They were the only people who mattered, the only people who should have been there, and I couldn't get hold of them. I needed them to see her, to appreciate how perfect she was, to tell me how like him she looked.

I leaned against the pay-phone and sobbed.

After the first two days of her life in a box she was allowed off the ventilator and into my arms that would always be warm enough.

'A mother's skin heats itself up if her baby is cold,' I was reliably informed. 'And if her baby is hot, it cools down.'

She kept trying to find my breast, her head bouncing up and down, face buried in my front as she dragged herself along, bounce bounce bounce, trusting that her little open mouth would land on a nipple soon. But when she finally arrived at the mountain it was, she just wasn't big enough. She couldn't suckle properly. I thought that it was my fault, that I was doing it wrong, but the doctor said that it was her, that she was too small to latch on. She would cry with frustration and I would do my best to comfort her. I would put her on my shoulder where she couldn't smell the milk, and I would rub her tiny bony back until she slept.

What I kept trying to understand was how they could have given me up. How in a million years and in a thousand variations of circumstance, any parent could ever give their child to anyone else. To complete strangers, no less. Vetted for suitability as surrogate parents by other strangers. To have and to hold, for better or for worse. Forever. Amen. How could they have let me go?

12

I had forgotten about Laura and Neil. I wasn't even sure that they were real any more, that anything about that family was real. Even Jack's death seemed so unlikely after she was born. All death seemed rather improbable, but Jack's above all else because, well, just look at her, how perfect she was. How much she expected of us all. As if no bad thing could ever happen in the world.

It soon became apparent, however, that Laura and Neil were all too real, because they came to collect us, long before we were at all fit to leave. 'Your brother and sister are here,' a nurse told me.

I had no idea who she meant. 'I'm an only child,' I said.

'That's funny,' she nodded, 'I thought you were. Me too.'

'So you must be wrong,' I explained.

'Well I don't know who they are,' she said. 'Only they did ask for you, and they did say they were – '

'What are their names?' I interrupted, feeling slightly uneasy.

'Don't ask me.'

'Well what do they look like, then?' I urged her impatiently.

'You'll see them in a minute, lovey, then you'll know.'

'But I don't want – '

Too late. Want or don't want. There they were. Standing in the doorway of our room. On the dot of visitor's hour. She had only been five days in the world, and they had already come for her.

I was in the same room, but two of the mothers had gone home that day, and the third one was sleeping. So I was on my own, more or less.

'Hello, Anna!' Laura exclaimed, rushing up and embracing me for the nurse to see. A real performance, almost convincing. 'How are you? You look radiant! Doesn't she look radiant, darling?'

She beamed at Neil, who smiled, possibly for the first time in his life. 'Absolutely radiant,' he said, turning his sickly grin on the nurse. 'And where's the little one?'

I felt the panic tighten like a vice in my gut. The nurse was about to leave the room, but I said, 'Don't go yet.' I couldn't think what else to say, not immediately.

She turned to look at me and frowned. 'What is it, lovey?'

'I – can you – I just need to . . .'

She came back to the bed. 'Need to what?'

I shot a glance at Laura and Neil. 'Sorry, would you mind waiting outside a minute?' I asked.

They darted their eyes at each other too fast, but in a fraction of a second they were smiling again and saying, 'Of course.'

The nurse looked very confused. 'Whatever is it?' she asked, almost within earshot of them, as if they were just relatives, nice and friendly.

'Get them out of here,' I said. 'Please.'

'Now that's no way to – '

'Get them out!' I pleaded. 'They'll kill her!'

She looked at me differently now, but not at all as if she understood. She looked at me as if she thought I had gone slightly mad. She patted my hand and said, 'Don't worry, lovey. Everything'll settle down soon, just you wait and see.'

I could see Neil's face peering in at us through the glass in the door. The nurse had her back to him.

'I want to speak to a policeman,' I whispered urgently.

'Now now now,' she cooed.

Then Neil pushed the door ajar and asked in a mild bright way if everything was all right.

'Fine,' I said coldly.

He stalled at the tone of my voice. 'Righto,' he nodded. 'Just checking up on you.' He closed the door again and glared at me through the glass.

'There now,' she said. 'He wouldn't hurt a fly.'

'If you let them go anywhere near her,' I warned, 'either of them, I promise you I'll kill you.'

Her expression suddenly turned very grave. 'When did you last see Professor Taylor?' she asked.

'Who's Professor Taylor?'

'Your consultant, lovey. Mike Taylor.'

'Oh, him. It's not him I need. It's the police I need,' I said. 'Can't you take that in?'

'I'll tell you what,' she said, 'I'll see if I can get the police along to see you, and you just wait right here.'

She had been sitting on the bed. She got up and marched towards the door, where Neil's face instantly disappeared from view. As soon as she was out in the corridor I could hear them both asking if I was all right, in hushed anxious tones.

'She's fine. Probably just the hormones,' I heard the

nurse explain. Had she taken me seriously then? I couldn't tell. She had taken something seriously, but I wasn't sure it was me.

And then I heard Laura say, 'Because she was acting very strangely even before the birth, I have to say. Very strangely.'

Then the nurse said something I couldn't hear. It sounded like a question, judging from the inflection, and then they all went away, out of my earshot. I leapt out of bed immediately and ran after them. But they were going in the wrong direction for Special Care, to my immense relief.

I stopped myself in my tracks. Tried to calm down. I realized how paranoid I must have sounded. In a way the nurse was right, it was the hormones. They made me feel so vulnerable, so utterly powerless, as if all I was good for now was love, and a very particular love, at that. Just for her. Everything else seemed too big and trivial. She was the whole thing. But I would have to put on a show of calm, at least, or nobody would believe a word I said.

I went along to Special Care myself, to keep vigil, and she was still there, of course she was, how could anyone be allowed to take her but me? She was sleeping as deeply as the sea, worn out with growing so much, breathing all on her own with her two young lungs.

'You'll be taking her home soon,' she told me, that kind woman who had introduced us five days ago. 'She's a real fighter. She's made up her birthweight already. The way you love her, she's better out than in.'

I should have been so glad, but all I could think was: Where? What home?

13

It was the following day. Ten o'clock in the morning. I was to be discharged after lunch, as soon as the paediatrician had checked over my babe. For imperfections. As if. I was told that my brother and sister-in-law would be more than happy to come and collect me, and when I tried calmly to explain that I didn't want them to, nobody heard me.

The only telephone number I could remember off the top of my head was Nicholas Drake's. And I could remember the number of our old flat too, of course, but I still had to remind myself that Jack wasn't there any more. I don't know why I didn't just call the police. I think perhaps I was as worried about my sanity as everyone else seemed to be. I was so suggestible. And, as usual, what I thought I had seen, thought I knew, seemed so unlikely after a good night's sleep.

I waited for the telephone. A new mother was crying to someone about her Day Three Blues, about the milk coming in and how sore she was with feeding, how hard it was, how her stitches hurt, how she couldn't poo, how she could hardly walk. Eventually she hobbled away, her legs so far apart that there might have been a volley-ball stuck between her thighs. I remembered Day Three, I thought, as if it were years ago. My own sleepy chick was snuffling at my breast as if born to it.

I dialled. He came on the line, as hurried as ever.

'Drake.'

'Nicholas. It's Anna.'

'Yup.'

'I've just had my baby.'

'Congratulations,' he said, a little disoriented. 'Boy or girl?'

'Girl.'

'Very nice. Girls are easier, I'm told.'

'Really? Do you have children?'

'I have boys. Two boys. They still wear me out and they're in their late twenties now.' A slight pause. 'What can I do for you?'

'I expect you'll laugh,' I began.

'I very much doubt it. I haven't time,' he said. 'Do be brief, if you can.'

'Very well,' I said, quietly so that nobody else could hear. 'To put it bluntly, I think Neil has done something awful to Max.'

Pause.

'By " awful", what exactly do you mean?'

'Something violent.'

A sharp intake of breath. 'Do you have any evidence to substantiate this claim?'

'Not yet. At least, I – '

'Have you informed the police?'

'No.'

'Why not?'

'I don't know why not. Because I – '

'You *don't know*?'

'All right, I do, I know exactly why not. I went into labour, for a start.'

I heard him mutter something inaudible to somebody else – his secretary, perhaps. 'Labour,' he repeated, returning his voice to the mouth-piece. 'Yes, of course.' He sounded as if he were concentrating hard after a major distraction. 'Could you be specific about the nature of Neil's violence, Anna?'

'I think Max is dead,' I said.

Complete silence. Even his breathing stopped.

'And also,' I went on, 'I'm beginning to wonder about all these other deaths, I don't mind telling you.'

'What other deaths?'

I couldn't believe that he was asking me. 'Look,' I said, 'I know I'm only small fry in your great scheme of things, now that George Stubbs the almighty has passed away, but I'm talking about murder here.'

'I'm a lawyer,' he said, 'not a policeman.'

'You're a human being, aren't you?'

'Not often,' he admitted. 'Only on my days off.'

'Well take a day off then, will you? Because this is very important.'

More silence.

'Are you listening to me, Nicholas?'

'Of course.'

'But are you really listening? Or are you just – '

'Do excuse me a moment, would you?' he said. And then the line went click.

I waited. It sounded as if I were on hold. I waited a long time. Eventually there was another click, and a ringing sound. And then his voice again, welcome as a friend's. An ally's voice in a war I was losing.

'Anna?'

'Nicholas.'

'Are you suggesting that Lord Stubbs, and his wife Clarissa, and your husband Jack were all murdered?'

'That's exactly what I am suggesting.'

'And furthermore, that Max may also have been murdered?'

'Yes.'

A pause. A slow breath, weighed down by *gravitas.*

'That is an extremely serious accusation,' he warned. 'I hope you have grounds for it. I hope it's not merely a whim.' He pronounced the 'h' in whim. 'Not just some hormonally induced hysteria,' he added. Insult to injury.

'Thank you so much for your confidence,' I said.

'Forgive me,' he insisted, 'but I have to be sure. Because I must now act upon what you have told me, and I would prefer not to seem ridiculous in the eyes of Scotland Yard for taking any notice of you.'

'Please act upon it,' I begged, losing my calm immediately. A split second of hope, and I was the epitome of hormonally induced hysteria. 'Please, Nicholas. They're coming to get me any minute now, and I'm so frightened. I think they'll try to kill me too. And my baby. You must – '

I stopped abruptly, because at that very moment I could see Neil walking through the security door into the post-natal ward. Followed closely by an artificially smiling Laura.

'Anna? Are you there?'

'Yes,' I said. 'I must go.' I replaced the receiver.

Laura waved to me, bright and friendly. I waved back, as if it were safe now, safe to go along with their game, even safe to go back to Barkwood with them. Help was on its way.

They waited in the TV room for most of the morning, taking no chances with me. I felt smug and cunning for having called Drake. It was quite clear that nobody in the hospital would take me seriously, but I knew that Drake would. I was safe at last. Soon they would be behind bars. They looked every inch her parents themselves with a new car-seat at their feet, waiting to collect her. They looked respectable. Coupled and clean. Appearances matter, I thought. If your soul is a mire, smile.

The paediatrician took forever to come but no time at all to decide that she was perfect. How could she not be? Weighing in at five pounds two, she was all that she should be and more. Precious beyond reason. Jack's.

I was checked over by Mike Taylor, the consultant. My stitches had been taken out the day before and my wound was healing nicely, he said.

'This pouch, Mike,' I said, 'what do I do with it?'

'Nothing at all for six weeks,' he smiled. 'No sit-ups or you're liable to burst. You've had a major operation, remember.'

My scar was like a blue plaque on an empty house: Here lived Wren, smallest of all small birds.

I got dressed. I noticed that I still looked pregnant. I had no luggage to speak of; two vests and one baby-gro that were gifts from other mothers to Wren. I slipped a clean vest over her tiny head. She looked very beautiful in white, her jaundice like a suntan, yellow as sand.

'Let her take a little sun every day through a window,' the paediatrician instructed me. 'Careful not to let her burn.'

I checked us both out at the desk, as if we had spent the week in a two-star hotel. For a fleeting moment I thought we might just be able to slip away without their noticing, but they were both beside me in no time, like armed body-guards, exchanging pleasantries with the nurses.

I was almost looking forward to what was in store for them. The shock on their faces, how it would satisfy me.

'A midwife will visit you every day for the first ten days,' I was told.

Neil shot a wary glance at his wife. She nodded her assent, almost inconspicuously. Ten days, I thought. Thank God for ten days. A thin safety-net, if Drake lets me down.

'But my wife's a midwife,' said Neil.

'Are you?' The girl at the desk beamed. 'Which hospital?'

'I'm independent,' she said quickly. Defensively. 'I'm not attached to any hospital.'

She was probably struck off, I thought.

'Not local then, or I'd know you, wouldn't I?' said the girl.

'I am local but I'm not working at the moment,' she said. 'I haven't practised for a while.'

The girl nodded, her interest waning. 'Looks like you'll have a double-whammy of after-care,' she said to me.

'I could keep a check on them both myself if you like,' Laura persisted. 'Fill in her notes, weigh her, keep an eye on Anna, the lot.'

'That's very kind,' said the girl at the desk, 'but you must know we can't do that if you're not her named midwife. She must see her named midwife, attached to this hospital. Thanks anyway.'

'Red tape, eh?' said Neil.

Good old red tape, I thought.

'Could you just sign here, then?' the girl asked me. I did. 'Have you seen your midwife this morning?'

I nodded.

'And you've got your notes for the baby?'

'I have.'

Wren was tiny in her car-seat, sitting in the front beside her uncle, as if she trusted him. He drove slowly, cautiously, all the way back to the middle of nowhere. Barkwood House. I began to feel very uneasy. Tired and helpless and quite at their mercy, or lack of it. Suppose help didn't come? Neil was almost tender, the way he took a bend in the road or slowed down behind a car. As if he were incapable of the slightest violence. Laura was sitting in the back with me. She was very preoccupied, just as she had been after the birth, as if she were trying to work out something very complicated. There was no show in her any more, no false smile. I had seen her for what she was, and she wasn't denying it. The trap was laid, as far as she was concerned. I had already nibbled at the bait. When she smiled at me now, it was far more unsettling because she meant it.

I hoped that the police would be waiting when we turned down the drive, but there was no sign of them. I began to worry. Weary worry, too tired for very much. My heart leapt involuntarily at the sight of Jack's car, waiting for his family, and then it sank again. Grief never goes, it grows. It matters most. You walk about with a wound for the rest of your life. I tried to remember where I had put the car-keys and, if I could find them, how I would position Wren if I couldn't steal the car-seat. But then I remembered that I wasn't allowed to drive for another five weeks and I felt hopeless. Afraid.

Neil switched off the engine. I said a silent prayer. The quiet chilled me, the isolation implicit in it. No one to shout to for help. I began to doubt Drake, even to suspect him of some intrigue with the two of them. Neil opened the back of the Land-Rover. The sun seemed very bright, but there was a refreshing breeze that soothed me after the long hot journey. I climbed out to fetch Wren but Neil was already there, swinging her car-seat like a shopping basket on one arm. I reached for her but he snatched her away and, instantly, the fear deserted me. I was furious. I felt immensely powerful, as if I had sufficient rage to overwhelm them both. 'I can manage,' he said, a strange mixture of courtesy and possessiveness in his tone.

'Be careful of the sun on her,' I insisted.

Her blue eyes were squinting in the brightness of it, but he took no care. 'Don't fuss,' he said.

She began to cry. I didn't feel frightened at all any more. Not of anything. I felt that if it came to it I could kill. If help didn't come, I was easily sufficient for her. Weak as I was, I could protect her from harm.

'I *said* be careful, Neil.'

'Crikey, if she can't even handle a bit of sun!'

Laura said, 'Of course she can't. She's only a week old.'

I took heart from this. Even if they kill me, I thought, she won't let him harm her.

Neil said, 'Tell that to a baby in Africa or India or – '

'Please Neil,' I said, the rage mounting in me, 'she's not even supposed to be born yet.'

He marched away towards the house, knocking the car-seat against him carelessly. She was sobbing convulsively, the way a baby does, as if the end of the world has come. She could hardly catch each breath between the howls. I thought of her immature lungs, of how they had only just learnt to draw in the air. I thought of what the woman had said about the way I loved her, how she was better out than in. And I thought, if he doesn't give her back to me she will die. Or I will kill him. I tore after him, but I was immediately pulled up short by my wound.

'Calm down,' said Laura behind me. 'Anna, calm down.'

So this is home, I thought. Welcome home, little bird.

I began to cry myself. For all of us. For her, for Jack, for Max, for me, even for Laura and Neil. For the fact of cruelty, how it wormed its formidable way into all of our lives, somehow. Cruel fate. Cruel minds. Cruel memories. Cruelty seemed then – and perhaps was – more real and unavoidable than any amount of love. And I felt that I had done her the greatest cruelty of all. I had brought her into being.

I felt Laura's arm around my shoulder. 'You're getting yourself into a terrible state,' she said.

We went into the house after him, her steps discreetly anxious next to mine, her arm still clutched around me, like fear. I wondered if it was really me that she was comforting.

I couldn't withstand my baby's cries any more. They screamed down the stairs for me as soon as I was in the hall. They would scream until I came, until I comforted her, until she could smell me again. I climbed the stairs as fast as I possibly could, my heart racing with rage at Neil for taking her from me. She kept on and on until the sound became intolerable, an animal sound that cut across all barriers, all continents, a scream like a screw turning in my heart, a cry in the wild, for her very survival. It wasn't literal, of course it wasn't, she wasn't about to die at that very moment, but she *felt* that she was, she felt so afraid. I couldn't help thinking of Max, of what he had said about surviving. And what Jack had said, too. Both of them. It was suddenly so obvious what they meant.

Neil had taken her out of the car-seat and put her in a cot. A brand new cot. She was lying on her back, kicking and waving her arms, like an insect turned upside down. He was standing over her, just looking. As if she didn't move him at all.

I pushed him away. 'Excuse me,' I said.

'How dare you push me,' he barked.

I picked her up in spite of him, in spite of the furious indignation of him that burned into me. Her sobbing subsided immediately, but she was still shaking, like someone in shock, someone who had just escaped death.

'This isn't even your house!' Neil shouted at me.

I put her to my breast but she couldn't latch on because of the sobbing still, because she could hardly breathe by now, because Neil was shouting. 'Who the hell do you think you are? Miss bloody Nobody!'

'Leave her alone,' Laura intervened.

'Don't tell me what to do!'

I think he hit her. It was that same sound anyway. A hand across a face. I walked away from them, out of the room they had prepared for her, on to the landing where the warm sun shone, down the stairs, out into the fresh breeze. I sang to her and stroked her funny little head until she was calm.

14

They left me in peace when I came inside again, out of the hot sun, but they argued on between themselves in clipped whispers. I couldn't hear a word they said, although if I look back now I can guess all too easily what they were negotiating.

I lay on my bed with her beside me, so tiny that I feared crushing her if I slept. But I had to sleep. I needed to, whenever she slept, or my brain would be a marshland to sink through, lucid thoughts swallowed up in a bog. A mire of feeling. No solid ground. And yet I couldn't, didn't dare, lay curled around her like a leaf, sheltering her soft life from harm.

I wondered where they had put Max, but my brain couldn't even accommodate what they might have done to him, let alone where they might have dumped him afterwards. How could it persuade itself down a path of such dark speculation, when her brand-new perfect life lay beside me in trust, hoping for so much?

Sleep, I kept telling myself. Sleep. Dream of the sea and the sand, and the vast expanse of the sky and all the continents of land. Dream of a God who loves, protects, defends. Dream of Jack. Bring him back. Let him guide me. But all I could see was his face behind my eyelids like an old photograph I never managed to take, caught at his most fine and full. At his most alive. But so frozen there.

She whinnied in her sleep like a galloping horse, chomping at the bit. Dreaming of roaming already. Breaking away too soon. I had the feeling that whenever she went would seem too soon. Even when she left one day behind to begin the next, it seemed too soon. I thought I would probably freeze her as well if I could, put her next to Jack in a double photograph frame. Safe.

Laura asked, through the door, if I was all right.

I told her I was sleeping, and she said, 'Good, that's good. You ought to sleep, you need to sleep, you really need to, Anna.'

I thought, so don't keep talking to me.

'We've been worried sick about you,' she said. 'You haven't been right since . . . well, ever since Jack died.'

I thought, you didn't even know me then. What are you talking about?

She asked if she could come in. Her voice had a bustling way about it, as if she had just come on duty, as if it were her shift.

I said I was half-asleep and I'd talk to her later.

'We're keeping an eye on you,' she warned.

'Well you don't need to,' I said. 'I'm fine.'

'You are not fine, Anna. You are ill. You're a prime candidate for PND.'

Please No Death, I thought.

She said, 'My advice to you, if you want to avoid it, is get a routine. Straight away. Four-hourly feeds, regular naps, down for the night at eight. Let her know who's boss.'

You're who's boss, I thought, by the sound of it.

'And all this breast-feeding lark,' she said, 'it's just a silly fashion thing. Take no notice. It's a fad.'

It's nature, I thought.

'They bang on about it these days as if it's the only way.'

Instinct. To suckle one's young.

'The sooner you get her on a bottle, the better.'

God's creation.

'If she'll take a bottle, I can help out. Make sure you get some proper rest.'

'Thank you Laura,' I said. 'I'd like to get some sleep now, if you don't mind.'

'Mind?' she exclaimed. 'I don't mind at all! That's what I'm asking you to do! That's what I'm saying to you.'

But something about what she was saying to me didn't add up.

'I'll knock at seven-thirty,' she stated, like a matron. 'That'll be the next feed. Then bath and bed.'

I couldn't face arguing.

'Have you changed her recently?'

I wondered if it was deliberate, this thing she was doing of keeping me awake. Like Japanese torture.

'Yes, thank you.'

'Good girl.' Pause. 'Got all you need?'

'I'm fine, thank you,' I answered too sharply, the edge in my voice cutting up the air. 'I'm quite capable of looking after her myself.'

Silence. 'I'm only trying to help,' she said.

'I know,' I agreed. But I didn't know, at all.

'There's no need to shout at me.'

'I'm sorry.'

Somehow I was to blame. Although she was torturing me. Somehow it was my fault.

And then I heard Neil say, 'Is she shouting at you?'

There was a cough, I don't know whose. And then, 'She's not well,' I heard Laura mutter, quite audibly. 'She really isn't well.'

Maybe I wasn't, I thought in earnest.

It was then that the police arrived. Or at least it was then that I became aware of them. I think, in fact, that they may have been there for some time, listening on the other side of the door.

'Anna, hello. My name is Black. DCI Black.'

DCI, I thought. Death Comes Inevitably.

'I wonder if I could have a quick word?'

I thought that it might be a trap, that if I opened the door, there would only be Laura and Neil standing there with weapons, ready for the next kill.

'Why should I believe you?' I said.

'I beg your pardon?'

'Why should I believe that you're who you say you are?'

'Because . . .' He hesitated, lost for words. 'Because I am.'

'But how do I know? How do I know you're not Neil, putting on a voice?'

'Because I'm Neil,' said Neil.

'And I'm Black,' said Black. 'I'll pass some ID under the door.'

ID, I thought. Inevitable Death.

A small plastic wallet thing came under the door. I didn't bother picking it up. I didn't want to wake her by moving about. Not just yet.

I said, 'I know what. Laura and Neil go downstairs and stand outside my window where I can see you.'

'Why?' asked Neil irritably.

'Just do it,' said Black, quietly and efficiently.

I heard footsteps clatter down the wooden stairs. I eased my chick on to my shoulder where she squawked until I settled her. I stood at the window and watched. They came round the side of the house, looking up at me anxiously. 'Are you still there?' I asked DCI Black.

'I most certainly am.'

I moved to the door and unlocked it. Someone else was standing beside him, and for a split second I thought it was Laura and that Black was Neil. I was expecting uniforms, and they were both in plain clothes.

'This is my colleague,' he said. 'Joanna Redmond.'

'Hello, Joanna. Come in.'

They did. I locked the door behind them again.

'Have a seat,' I said hospitably.

He was a smallish man in early middle-age, very tight and compact. Not a lot of hair. His face was round and kind but worried. It wore the lines of inhabited stress, as if stress was a home he was almost comfortable in. Like his creased suit. Joanna was tall and red-haired and rather beautiful. My age, at a guess.

I stood at the window, keeping an eye on the chief suspects. 'Did Drake call you then?' I asked.

I wasn't feeling easy with them. Either of them. I didn't know why. I should have felt so relieved, so safe at last, but I didn't. I felt suspicious. All I could think was, what have they told them? What lies have they told?

'That's right,' said Black. 'A Mr Nicholas Drake.' He was looking at his note-pad to make sure.

'Yes, well, there's a body somewhere here,' I declared, getting straight to the point. See if they meant business or not. 'I've no idea where. I don't expect they'll tell you, will they? You'll just have to find it.'

'Who's "they"?' asked Joanna Redmond.

'Them,' I said. 'Those two.'

'Neil and Laura Stubbs?' she asked.

'Who else?'

Black looked very thoughtful and grave. 'And whose body is it?' he asked kindly.

'What?' They were coming too fast, and I was too tired.

'Whose body do you believe is here, that you propose we find?'

'Max's body,' I said. 'It's Max. Didn't he tell you that?'

'Who?'

'Drake.'

A meaningful look passed between them, but the meaning was all theirs. I could only guess at it. If I wasn't so tired . . .

'And Max is,' he studied his pad again, 'your brother-in-law?'

'My other brother-in-law, not that one,' I explained, nodding towards Neil.

'No,' he said soberly. 'Obviously not that one. That one seems very much alive and well.'

I felt ridiculous, and must have seemed it. But I couldn't begin to explain to him, in the jumble of everything, how frightened and anxious I was.

'I wonder if you could be very specific now, Mrs Stubbs, about your grounds for suspicion?' he asked.

'Aren't you going to take me to the police station?' I asked.

'We certainly will need an official statement, yes,' he said. 'But if you – '

'I saw him. Those are my grounds. Wrapped up in a sheet. I saw them carry him into their car and drive him up to the house. And then I saw him here. On the floor here.'

I pointed to the exact spot.

They both looked at the floor, as if half-expecting to see Max there. 'And they were in here too, when I came in. When I found him. They were trying to kill me too. I honestly think they were. They nearly did, only I went into labour.'

He nodded, but there was more kindness than credence in his expression. 'It's a very serious allegation you're making, Mrs Stubbs.' He spoke as if to a child.

'I know,' I replied in my most grown-up voice. 'And I'm very seriously making it. I think they killed Max, and I think they killed Jack. I don't know about Clarissa and George. I really don't know about them.'

They looked at each other again.

'Clarissa and George are your parents-in-law, is that right?' asked Black.

'*Were*,' I corrected. 'They're both dead now.'

'I do apologize. Were. And you have grounds for finding both of their deaths suspicious, do you?'

'Not grounds, no. Not for them.'

'And for Jack's death?' asked Joanna.

'Only a feeling,' I said, feeling it instantly.

'Jack was your late husband?' she asked. 'Is that right?'

Too late, I thought.

'Mrs Stubbs?'

'I got there too late,' I said. I could feel the old grief

surfacing again, the same old disbelief of grief. 'He was already dead, you see. He was just hanging there. Dead. There was absolutely nothing I could do.'

She reached out to touch my arm.

'Was there?' I pleaded.

'No there wasn't,' she said, very calmly, very clearly. 'There was nothing at all you could do. He was already dead.'

'There was absolutely nothing I could do,' I repeated to Black.

I tried to sit on my grief, to somehow rein it in, so that I could sound calm, but I was weeping uncontrollably, and there was nothing I could do about that either.

'I loved him,' I said.

'Of course you did.'

'And he loved me, you see. He wouldn't have done it,' I explained.

'Perhaps he – '

'He wouldn't have left me. He simply wouldn't have done.'

'Perhaps he left you for other reasons,' said Black.

'Don't you understand what I'm saying?' I shouted at him. 'He wouldn't have done it!'

She woke up on my shoulder and started crying with me. We were both out of control, both lost without him. Both lost now.

'It's all right,' said Joanna. But it wasn't. 'You're going to be all right. You're both going to be all right.'

'I saw Max!' I shouted at Black through my tears. 'I saw him dead!'

'I'm very sorry,' Black explained, 'but you can't have done. Max is alive and well.'

'What?' I demanded. 'Where?'

'Why don't you make an appointment to see your GP?' Joanna suggested as she climbed into the car.

'I don't have a GP.'

'Then I suggest you get one,' she said. 'Ask your midwife to fix one up for you.'

Black turned the key in the ignition.

'You'll be sorry,' I warned them, 'if you leave me, today. With them. You'll be back in no time looking at my corpse.'

They frowned at each other, but not because they took me seriously, I could tell that much. More likely because they didn't take me seriously. I think they were worried, like Mum and Dad were, wondering what they could say that would make sense to me.

'And she'll be dead too,' I said, holding her up in the sun for them to adore. 'If you can live with that on your conscience.'

Laura and Neil came round the side of the house at the sound of the car engine ticking over. They were waving in that friendly way of theirs. Black nodded at them neatly, as if any suspicion he might have felt had to be contained within a capsule of courtesy.

'Any worries,' he said quietly, leaning across his colleague, 'call. Ask for me.'

I watched them drive away. My lifeline, slipping out of my grasp. There was nothing else I could do.

15

I went back into the house, locking myself in my room like an adolescent child. I even closed the shutters. Armour against their power over me. I found my address book, at last, and telephoned Mum and Dad. No answer.

Her nappy was full, smelling of yoghurt. It was the colour of liquid yellow ochre, her tiny bony bottom stained with it, like a big nicotine stain. I changed her and fed her and we both lay down for a while. She snuffled and whinnied in her sleep again, roaming on. I kept kissing her head with its silky coating of down like a mouse's back.

I thought about Jack, tried to retrieve him, pretend that he was still alive. I rummaged through my memories, sticking them so close together that they ran like a film.

I'm at a private view. A friend's exhibition of photographs. Innocence and Experience, it is called. Mostly portraits. Faces that suffer and faces that don't. A great divide, as if there were no middle ground. It irritates me. It is like a gimmick. I don't know the artist well. Jeff, he's called. I'm not even sure that I like him very much. He's cynical and greedy and quite hard-nosed. I persevere with him because my best friend loves him and may even marry him one day. And I love her. I think, even so, that if she does marry him I'll hardly ever see her, so my efforts are probably in vain. He doesn't like me either, I've no doubt about that. He thinks I'm a bad influence on her, that she spends too much time with me, that I'm some kind of threat. He's already winding me up, everything he says and does like nails on a blackboard, and I've only been here for half an hour. But I'm thirty today and it's Saturday night and I want to be out on the town. I'm looking at a photograph of someone I know. I know him quite well, I'm sure, but I can't think who he is. And I can't decide if he has a suffering face or the face of innocence. His expression is strangely neutral.

Josie says, 'What do you think?' She's standing behind me so that I don't have to look at her when I lie. I say I like them, they're very interesting. She can read me like a book if she wants to, but she knows it's my birthday so she doesn't want to. She wants to pretend things are fine.

She says, 'What's that one, do you think? Innocence or experience?' Then I do look at her, because I love her, I love it that we're so alike. 'I really can't decide. Can you?'

She shakes her head. 'He won't tell me. He knows all their life histories, these subjects, but they're all in confidence. You just have to guess.'

It seems such a silly idea. So typical of him. I look away from her in case she sees my contempt as it travels across my face.

I say, 'I think he's either completely traumatized or totally bored.'

And then I notice that Jack is standing beside me without recognizing me, and I realize that it's him. The photograph. It's Jack.

'Bored,' he says.

And then he looks at me and smiles, but there's something cross in the lines around his mouth, as if the portrait angers him. And then he stops smiling altogether and says, 'Anna. Good God.'

'I knew I knew who you were,' I say ridiculously.

He says, 'How extraordinary.' He seems quite overcome.

'Josie,' I say, 'this is Jack. Josie is my best best friend.'

'Hi,' she says.

'Hi,' he agrees.

They shake hands, more or less. At least they go through the motions. But he hardly even looks at her really, he just sort of nods in acknowledgement and then looks back at me. So she slips away tactfully, making faces at me that he can't see. Girlhood faces, giggly and mischievous, suggesting a host of glorious things. Heaven, at last. Angels, archangels, joy. I frown at her but she just does it more so I stop looking at her altogether and look at Jack instead.

He says, 'Are you still in love with Max?'

I cringe inside, minding that he ever knew, wondering if Max knew too. 'You've no idea what agony it was,' he says. He's smiling still, a great wide grin across his face, all the anger gone. 'I was desperately unhappy, the whole summer long.'

'Were you? Why?'

'Why, she says! Why! My heart was bleeding for you, Anna. Didn't you know?'

'I had no idea.'

'Wasn't it obvious as day?'

'Honestly. No.'

'I can't believe it. I knew who your heart was bleeding

for. Every stupid piddly thing Max said, you'd laugh your head off. And then I'd say something profound and serious to show you how mature I was and you'd just stare blankly at me. Then Max would make some joke at my expense and you'd laugh your head off again.'

'Oh dear,' I say. 'How awful.'

'I vowed never to be serious again. I swear. It's been my life's work. Make women laugh.'

And I'm laughing as he speaks, but it's not what he's saying so much as the way he's saying it. That big expanse of smile, like arms opening. And also I'm embarrassed and flattered and quite excited and I'm trying to hide it all. So I'm laughing.

'Look!' he grins. 'I'm doing it!'

I thought I could hear Laura outside the door. Or was it Neil? Both of them perhaps. Waiting for their moment. Creeping about on the creaking floorboards. I wondered how they could really go through with it now. After the police had been. Whether the police believed me or not, they would believe me if I was dead. Couldn't they see that?

But then the noise went away, and I fell asleep.

I dreamt that she nearly died. I was on a boat with lots of people having a party. Jack was there. We left her for a minute to walk and talk along the deck. And then suddenly there was a great big wave that swept us all away. When the rescue people arrived, there was only her to save. Everyone else could swim.

We waited forever while they dived, hearts in our mouths, knowing that she couldn't survive. But they found her. They cupped her in their big hands and brought her over to us. She was only two inches long. She was sealed in plastic covering like a new toy. She looked very dead. She didn't move at all for twenty-five minutes. Her eyes were glazed over and open like dead eyes are. But eventually she stretched her arms a little and coughed up some sea water. So I took her out of the covering that must have saved her, and she wriggled about like a fairy in the palm of my hand. She was laughing and laughing and dancing about for joy.

But when I woke up, she was crying.

When I meet Jack the next weekend he's in the wars. He's broken one arm and he's wearing a neck-brace and he walks with a limp. We're supposed to be walking up the river from Hammersmith along the tow-path. It doesn't look promising.

'Fell off a scaffold,' he says.

I believe him. Why shouldn't I?

He says, 'If we've got a future, you and I, you'd better get used to this. I'm accident-prone. Give me a door and I'll walk right into it.' He's laughing about the fact, as if he's famous for it, as if it's all part of his charm. There's nothing about it that really alarms me. 'I cut myself with anything sharp, I throw myself off ladders, and I burn myself with anything hot.' He pauses, and then roars with laughter. 'Sorry about that.'

I'm laughing with him, although it isn't funny really. I'm laughing because he's so like Max used to be, and because I'm happy, because he's here.

'Crap, that exhibition, wasn't it?' he says plainly.

I might even love him already. Clear as water. Refreshing as water. 'Well it's not – '

'Or is Jeff your boyfriend?' he interrupts, this second thought worrying the muscles around his mouth.

'Jeff? God, no.'

'Good.' He takes my arm, as if it belongs to him. 'Well I have to, don't I?' He grins impishly. 'I'm a cripple. Have mercy.'

He limps along beside me. We look so silly. It's our first date. It's meant to be romantic, but all we can do is laugh.

'The thing about Jeff Shue is,' he says, 'he can't take photographs. So he always has to have some poncey little theme around them to hide the fact.'

I wonder now. About that scaffold. Whether he really fell or whether he jumped. But he was happy at that time, even if he was unhappy when he died. Even if he did kill himself. So why would he want to jump?

It occurred to me that Jeff Shue might know, that Jack might really have gone along with the exhibition idea and told him his story. Which was why he was so cross about it afterwards.

I promised myself that when I was strong enough to escape from their grasp, I'd take my bird on my back and find Jeff Shue and turn a screw in him until he told me. And Josie could help, whether she liked it or not. Out of guilt. Because she owed me. Jack's life history.

We've been together four months. We're on holiday in the Dordogne. Staying in a rented farmhouse with Mum and Dad. We're walking through the market-place at St Alvère. Buying bread and goat's cheese and ripe peaches for lunch. It's only our second day there. Mum walks with a hand on my shoulder all morning, just out of love. Dad is telling Jack about that cottage we rented in Devon, all those summers ago, how happy we were. Jack has a look of bewilderment in his eyes, and his mouth seems a little shaky when he tries to speak.

Then we're sitting in the courtyard of the farmhouse in the hot midday sun. We're drinking a delicious white wine and eating everything we bought. Dad is in the middle of opening a third bottle when Jack says to me, quite loudly, 'Maybe it's because you're adopted.'

'What?' I ask.

'The way they are with you.'

They can both hear perfectly clearly what he's saying, even though he's just talking to me. They're frowning as hard as I am, trying to understand what he means.

'What way is that, Jack?' Mum asks him.

She has such a kind inquisitive way of asking things, it's hard to refuse her. Her face is all soft with curves; she tilts it gently to one side to catch you off-guard. You can feel her trying to see into your soul.

Jack looks at her in surprise, as if her question is almost rude, an invasion of his privacy. I think he's a bit pissed. He seems quite angry, but in a harmless, affable way. Angry about something remote. He says, 'Nothing really. No particular way. It's not important.'

He pauses, gulping at the glass of wine that Dad has just filled. 'Just how you are with her, that's all. It's nice to see. Unusual.'

And then he laughs it off, and does one of his big wide grins that makes you feel warm inside. So that you forget what he's said. You just want to bask in the glow of his smile and forget the darkness in him. It's a trick of his, a way of deflecting. It soon stops working on me.

She woke up again, her blue eyes wide open, staring at me in astonishment, as if she'd only just noticed me. She smiled, I swear she did, and then she threw up. All over me. And then she smiled again. Just like Jack would. I couldn't help laughing, which puzzled her. She frowned and then smiled and then threw up again.

'I love you,' I said, which she understood perfectly.

Laura knocked on the door to tell me that it was half past seven now. I didn't say anything. I wanted her to leave me alone.

'Did you hear me, Anna?'

I didn't answer. She tried to open the door. 'Anna? I know you're in there.'

'What?'

'Max is here,' she said. 'Do you want to see him?'

'No.' I didn't believe her for a moment. I thought it was the most ridiculous way of trying to get access to me.

But then a voice said, 'Anna? It's me,' and it really sounded like Max. 'Can I see your baby?' he begged. 'I'm dying to see her. Is she beautiful?'

I tried to check through the key-hole to see how they were doing it, with a tape-recorder or something, but they were standing too close to the door.

All I could see were somebody's trousers.

'It's no good,' said Laura. 'She won't come out. I don't know what to do.'

I heard them walk away along the corridor.

The room was beginning to smell a bit rancid. Of old yoghurt-and-urine-filled nappies, stuffed into a plastic bag. She needed changing again already. I was running out of space. I opened the shutters and emptied the bag of nappies out of the window on to the lawn at the back.

The shit had gone everywhere. Up her back and out past her thighs, staining her tiny vest. I started to cry and then she started and then I couldn't stop. My tears fell over her little limbs as if they were washing her.

16

Early next morning. The distant noise of tapping again. A small but insistent sound, like someone knocking on a door. I decided to see what it was. I thought I had a fairly shrewd idea. I thought it was probably Neil trying to bury Max. I wanted to catch him. I wanted evidence. I even took Jack's Leica.

I crept out of bed without disturbing my chick and unlocked the bedroom door. I stood in the doorway like a sentinel at my post, listening out. It seemed that the noise was coming from downstairs. A weak sound really, but so regular, as if whoever it was had endurance, even if he had no strength.

I wondered whether to lock her in. I worried about not hearing her if the door was closed. I hovered uncertainly, thinking that perhaps I should take her instead. And then I thought, if I take her and she cries, she'll give us both away. So I left her there, the door open as far as it would go.

No sign of anyone in the hall. No lights on. A creeping feeling of loneliness blowing through me like cold air. I thought I almost preferred enemies to such loneliness. Even Laura, or Neil. Someone to give me an edge, however hard; a boundary to myself, somewhere to stop.

Passing Max's old room, I noticed that his door was open too, and that the bed was unmade. I didn't dare to switch on the light. I just stood in the doorway trying to see what I could. It looked as if he had just slipped out to the loo for a pee. It looked as if he was really alive after all, warm with sleep. As if the noise might be his. I went in and felt the sheets for some trace of human heat, but my hands recoiled with cold.

I'd got used to his death, in a way. You can get used to anything if it happens enough.

The stairs creaked undisguisably. I paused with each step to hear if I had been heard, to hear if she had stirred, to hear that no one had noticed me. Then on. Keep on. A journey that I would skip through in daylight, but in the dark it was like wading through thick water, syrupy and heavy and slow.

The tapping stopped.

I waited, suspended. Directionless. I kept wondering if I had done the right thing, leaving her alone upstairs.

Then the tapping started again. Perhaps whoever it was had heard me, or thought they had, and then decided that they hadn't after all, and resumed their business.

I resumed mine. One final step and I was in the hall at last, away from the creaking wood. I stood still on the stone floor, the cold of it numbing my feet. I was trying to get my bearings. From where I was standing, it sounded as if the noise was still beneath me, down yet another flight of stairs, if there was one. I lay on the stone and put my ear to the ground. The sound stopped immediately, as if whoever it was could hear me clearly now, could even see me perhaps, was maybe expecting me. As if I had walked into a trap that was just waiting for me.

I stayed as still as I could, fumbling with the lens on Jack's Leica, trying to be ready in time. I had never used it before, I realized, and it was proving a mystery. I didn't even know if it had a film in it.

And then suddenly the front door flung open, and Max walked in. He didn't see me lying on the floor, and I had no time to warn him. He tripped over me and hit his head on the newel post. 'Jesus Christ! What the fuck was that?'

He was on his feet again in no time, standing over me, reaching for the light in the hall. I had my hands over my head in fear, expecting a blow, but I could see the light through my fingers, and I could see Max staring down at me in shock.

'Please God no,' he muttered.

I think he thought I was dead. I could hear her crying upstairs, but my muscles felt paralysed. I was so terrified, I could hardly move. He bent down next to me and prodded me gently. 'Anna?'

'I'm OK.'

'God.' He exhaled audibly. 'God, you gave me a fright.'

I didn't have the words for the fright he had given me, or if I did, they were unspeakable above her howls. I still had my hands over my face, clamped there like rigor mortis.

'What were you doing, lying on the floor?'

'Nothing,' I said. 'I don't know.'

He frowned. 'Here,' he said kindly, taking my hands from my face. 'Let's get you on your feet. Sounds like she needs you.'

She was sobbing uncontrollably. I was failing her for

every second that I wasn't there, by her tiny side, holding her tight and safe.

'How come you're here, Max?'

'I – I was just – outside,' he stumbled. 'I was walking. Couldn't sleep.'

'No, I mean, here? *Alive.*'

'I'm sorry?' He was trying to get me up from the floor, and his face was staring at mine, full of concern.

'I thought you were dead,' I said.

'Anna,' he said very gravely, 'do you think you might have – '

'Don't even say it,' I snapped.

I was suddenly very nervous that they were right.

He didn't say it. He didn't say anything. He helped me up the stairs, half-carrying me, as if he shared my sense of urgency about comforting her and had the means I lacked. He sat me down on the bed and picked her up immediately, so tenderly, as if he loved her too.

'Be careful of her head,' I said.

But he knew about babies' heads, and hers was safe in his hands. He put her in my arms, but she couldn't feed at all, not until she had told me exactly what she had been through, as if I might not have heard her from the beginning, as if I didn't know. I had to rub her tummy to calm her down before she could latch on.

'She's beautiful,' he said.

I said, 'She looks like Jack.'

He smiled. 'Can I get you some water?'

How did he know about water?

'Everyone knows about water in Italy,' he explained, as if I had said it out loud. 'Extended families . . .'

He bent down and kissed her little head while she fed. For a fleeting moment his cheek was against my breast, and he seemed to be part of us all, as if he belonged too. Him and me and Jack and her. All together. And then he hurried off to get the water.

I drank it all. He had to get me another two glasses.

'It suits you,' he smiled. 'Motherhood.'

I didn't think that now was the time for compliments. 'I thought you were dead, Max.'

'Yes.' He paused thoughtfully. 'So you said.'

'I *saw* you dead. I saw them carry you.'

'Carry me?'

'Oh come on. Don't try and tell me I imagined the whole bloody thing!'

'I'm sorry, Anna. I don't know what you're talking about.' He seemed genuinely puzzled. 'What whole thing?'

My mind was scanning memories for some kind of certainty. Some tangible thing that I could point to. That. Explain that.

The whole event replayed itself in front of me, indelibly imprinted in my mind's eye, every split second of it. From the drive to the cottage to the house to hospital. I saw it. I did. I know I did.

So why was he lying to me?

'Never mind,' I said. 'I must have dreamt it.'

'Unless . . .' he began but didn't finish.

'Unless what?' I was grasping at straws, but it wasn't even straw, as it turned out.

'Unless you're . . . ill,' he said.

I didn't bother to defend myself. I wasn't sure any more.

'Are you, do you think?'

'You do, clearly.'

'I don't know. I don't know what the symptoms are. You do seem – odd.'

'I thought you were dead! I've had a baby!' I screamed. 'You'd seem odd.'

He nodded, trying to reassure himself more than me. 'I'm sure I would.'

We sat in silence like two small islands, oceans between us. He reached out to stroke Wren's head while I winded her, as if to comfort someone at least.

'Have your parents seen her?'

She belched loudly.

'No.'

'You've told them, though?'

I shook my head. She flopped to sleep on my shoulder. He frowned. 'But I thought you – loved them?'

'I've had other things to think about.'

'But she's their grandchild.'

'Not in blood.'

'Who cares about blood? Love is what's important! They love you!'

'I thought you were dead!' I shouted at him.

I felt my face go. The muscles pulled at it in spasms of sorrow, more tears washed through. I began to wonder if I was only at the beginning of grief, if I had even begun the long journey.

He looked surprised by something, but he didn't say what.

'Shall we tell them in the morning?' he suggested kindly.

He was trying to put his arm around me, I noticed,

but he didn't seem to know how. So tentative. Like a pubescent boy. The one I fell for so many summers ago. He pawed at my shoulder instead, more like a dog than a man.

'Do I matter so much to you?' he asked, finally.

But I wasn't sure who it was, any more, that mattered so much to me. I couldn't answer him. I had more questions than answers. So much uncertainty.

'What were you doing outside, Max?'

'I was . . . just . . .' I sensed that he was about to lie, but then thought better of it. The colour drained from his face and he put his hand over his mouth. 'I think I'm going to be sick,' he said.

He retched like a dog, but it was a very dry heave, thankfully.

'The coffins. I – I've been – I . . .'

A violent feeling of nausea crept up my own throat and fell down to my stomach again. 'Jesus, Max.'

'I know.' He swallowed another heave. 'It's taken me forever to dig them up.'

The tapping noise, I thought.

'It's been – so – h-horrible.'

I didn't want to know. It was a step too far into the dark. His ivory face looked so drawn in the moonlight. Shadowed. Harrowed. Too pale. It seemed to be imploring me. Bear this with me. Please. Let me tell.

'I had to be sure,' he justified. 'For my own peace of mind.'

I thought that there were probably better ways to find peace of mind, but I didn't say so.

'It's difficult to see very much, even with a torch,' he

said. 'You have to k-keep – sort of – p-pulling back from the – from the – smell.' His hand was over his mouth again. 'And – well, God – no love lost between us, but she – she's my mother, you know.'

He swallowed. Wren snored. I tried in spite of myself to imagine the smell. 'She looks f-fairly bashed about, but I don't know what's decay,' – his hand at his stomach now – 'or what's injury.'

'And – George?' I asked unwillingly. 'What was – left of him?'

'He isn't there.'

'Not at all?'

'No. His coffin was empty.'

'How odd.'

'That's what I thought.'

'Nothing there at all?'

He shook his head. 'There was just his old pocket-watch in there. Still – ticking.' He took it out of his own pocket to show me. 'Where are the charred remains that they said they buried?'

It didn't make sense. Even if it was murder. 'Who told you about the remains?' I asked.

'Drake did, I think. Unless it was you. Was it you?'

I couldn't remember.

'Who told you?' he asked.

'Laura told me.'

He shook his head again. 'Why would she lie?' he said. 'Unless . . .'

'Unless what?'

'Unless he's not dead at all.'

17

Laura got to the midwife at the top of the drive. She must have been waiting for her. I saw her leaning into the car window as I was coming back from the bathroom, clean at last. Clean hair. Clean everything. I thought that if I washed myself, looked presentable, I might argue a better case for my sanity. I couldn't help noticing the urgency with which she was gesticulating at the midwife through the car window. It was a new car. A dark-blue BMW. Expensive for a midwife. Maybe her husband is rich, I thought.

Laura talked to her for a very long time before the car drove on towards the house. And then she followed on foot. She was like a terrier. Once her teeth were in she wouldn't let go.

Max was eating breakfast downstairs. Neither of us had slept at all. It was already six o'clock by the time we went back to bed. And then Wren woke at six-thirty and wanted to talk. I did my best to listen, but she wanted a dialogue and it was hard to sustain. Everything ached. Head, limbs, heart. And then just as I was getting going, she went straight back to sleep. As soon as I was thoroughly awake.

I picked her up without waking her and joined Max downstairs. I found it almost unbearable to be apart from him, even in the same house. As if I couldn't afford to let him out of my sight any more. As if any separation were dangerous for us both.

I needed to tell him this. There was so much I needed to say to him.

He looked up from his toast as soon as we entered the room, concern across his face like a rash. His expressions had grown so much more revealing, as if his face had thawed out. I had hoped that our hours apart would have given him the chance to reflect on how sane I was, but I only had to look at his face to know differently.

'How are you?' he said, trying to sound ordinary.

'The midwife's coming,' I said. 'And Laura, of course. Like a bloody foot-soldier, keeping guard.'

He laughed. I wasn't joking.

'Don't go anywhere, will you?' I begged.

He frowned. 'Not if you don't want me to.'

'I really don't. I don't want you to go anywhere without me ever again.'

He looked a little taken aback. 'All right,' he agreed. He was humouring me. I didn't like it.

'If she makes me see the GP,' I said, 'will you take me? I don't want to go with them.'

'Of course I'll take you.'

'Can you drive?'

There was a loud knock. Wren woke up on my shoulder and started to cry.

'I'll go,' said Max. 'You just relax.' He stood up, swallowing the last of his toast and gulping his coffee down.

'Don't treat me like an invalid, Max. I'm OK,' I said. 'I'm not ill.'

'If you say so.'

'Please believe me.'

He looked as if he wanted to so much.

There was another loud knock and he was gone. I sat down. Tried to seem composed. I couldn't hear what they were saying above her cries. I thought I could hear Laura's voice. And then I heard Max say, 'She's just through here,' and a woman I didn't know followed him into the room.

'Hello Anna. I'm Dr Perry.' She put down her briefcase, held out a hand and smiled. She was small and neat and dark. She looked very efficient, with just a light covering of humanity on her, like a summer jacket. Easy to take off.

'I didn't ask to see you,' I said.

'No,' she agreed. 'Your relatives did. Everyone seems a little concerned about you.'

'I'm fine,' I said, digging my own grave.

'Good.' She smiled, turning to Max. 'I wonder if you might be so kind as to leave us alone for a while?'

'I don't mind if he stays,' I said.

And then Laura came in and I wondered how I could arrange it so that Max stayed and Laura went away.

'Just Max.'

'Very well,' said Dr Perry, still smiling. She glanced at Laura who obediently disappeared. Dr Perry closed the door behind her.

'How's the little one?' she asked, sitting down beside me.

'Fine.'

'What's his name?'

'Wren. She's called Wren.'

'Sorry. She.' Pause. 'Unusual name.'

I think she wrote it down. She wrote something down.

'And how have you been feeling?'

'Fine,' I said. 'Just a bit tired, that's all.'

She nodded. 'I know what it's like. I've got three of my own.'

She wrote something else down too. And then she looked hard at me and asked in her kindest voice yet, 'Are you feeling depressed at all?'

The tears pricked at my eyes instantly.

Max said that he thought I had every reason to feel depressed, and didn't she agree? He was trying to be on my side, but it felt like treachery.

'My husband killed himself six months ago,' I explained. She didn't even blink. 'I've just had his baby. She looks the spitting image of him. I think I'm grieving.'

'Wouldn't you be grieving?' Max demanded.

She ignored him, nodding at me as if she already knew what I had told her, as if Laura had prepared her for it. As if it were nothing much. 'It's a potent combination of life events,' she said.

I didn't understand what she meant. I thought she was prescribing me drugs.

'A death in the family, a baby, moving house, it's all quite a lot to take, a lot to come to terms with.'

'There's been more than one death in the family,' said Max. 'The whole bloody lot of them have been wiped out.'

Dr Perry ignored him. 'Are you feeling very weepy, very tearful?' she asked, as if they were different things.

'Not really,' I lied.

'Are you seeing things at all? Any hallucinations or – '

'Hallucinations?' Max pounced on the word. 'Are they a symptom?'

'They can be,' she said.

'A symptom of what? I haven't got anything,' I snapped.

'There's something called Puerperal Psychosis,' she explained, 'which can be very dangerous if it isn't treated. Sufferers often inflict harm on themselves and, more worryingly still, on their babies.'

'What's the treatment?' asked Max.

I was beginning to hate him.

'Hospitalization, almost without exception. Drugs. Therapy.'

'I won't go back to hospital,' I said.

'It's a very serious condition, Anna,' she warned, 'if you are suffering.'

I felt panicky again. Utterly alone. As if everyone was conspiring against me. Even Max. 'If I go to hospital, Laura will try and steal her,' I whispered.

She tried not to show how surprised she was. 'Steal who?'

'Wren.'

Silence. She looked at Max. He didn't do anything with his face, he just looked back.

'Why would she want to do that?'

'I don't know. Maybe because she wants a baby,' I said.

Dr Perry looked very grave. She was writing things down again. 'You don't think she'd just go ahead and have her own baby if she really wanted one?'

'It's not that simple. Is it, Max?'

'Isn't it?' he asked.

'You know it isn't!' I was almost shouting at him.

'Why isn't it that simple, Anna?' asked the doctor, quietly.

'Because of the will. Obviously.'

She looked at Max again. He shook his head.

'What will is that?'

'The will!' I repeated, as if there were only one. 'Because if I'm pregnant with Jack's baby, I inherit the house.'

'So? I don't follow,' she said. 'How does Laura wanting a baby make any difference to that?'

'Because if *they* have a baby and I don't, or if they steal mine, or if they pretend that I can't look after her, and if Max is dead, which he nearly was, and they make out that I'm mad, or if they kill me too, then *they* inherit the house.'

She wasn't even listening. She was staring deep into my eyes but she wasn't hearing a word I said. 'It sounds very complicated,' she said.

'It is. Very complicated. Isn't it, Max?'

He was smiling through a hard frown, trying to be supportive.

'Tell me something,' I asked him. 'Just tell me this. Did we stay up last night talking about your parents? About how they – died?'

'You know we did.'

'And have we had many conversations since I came here, about whether Jack was murdered or whether he took his own life?'

'Yes,' he conceded. 'We have.'

Dr Perry shot a nervous look at him.

'So I haven't imagined that?'

'No.'

'So why should I imagine that Laura wants to steal Wren?'

He shrugged. 'I don't know,' he said. 'I really don't know.'

'Exactly.' I was glaring at him, as uncomprehending as he was.

I thought back to that first morning there. Laura at the bedroom door. The way she asked me if I was pregnant. The cloud across her face. 'I know what I know,' I muttered.

'Like you know I was dead?' asked Max, dryly.

'Whose side are you on?'

'It's not about sides, Anna. It's about you, about whether or not you're well. I love you,' he said. 'I want you to be well.'

'I'm sorry, can we just back-track there?' said Dr Perry. 'You thought you saw him dead?'

I love you.

'Anna?'

'Yes?'

'You thought you saw him dead?'

'Yes.'

I love you.

'What did you see?'

I tried to concentrate. I thought that she was beginning to take me seriously, at last. 'I saw him wrapped up in a sheet. I thought he was dead, but obviously he wasn't. Perhaps he was just unconscious. Drugged or something. Then I saw them drag him out of their house and put him in the back of their car.'

She breathed in deeply as if she were meditating.

Max was frowning again.

'And you say this didn't happen, Max?'

'If it did, I have absolutely no recollection of it.'

A long pause hung on in the air.

'I think I would feel happier, Anna, if you would agree to see a psychiatrist.'

'A what? Are you mad?'

'How do you feel about that?'

'Do something, Max,' I begged.

'A psychiatrist?' he repeated dumbly. 'Are you sure that's necessary? Couldn't you treat her yourself?'

18

The psychiatrist admitted me to a hospital that specialized in my condition, or was about to, or thought that it might. In fact it was doing no such thing. It just wanted me there out of curiosity.

I was fairly sure that I didn't have a condition, but the more that people thought I did, the more uncertain I became. It was as if they couldn't hear me. Like talking through thick glass. Like prejudice must feel, when a person has already made up their mind. You're wasting your breath, there's no point in trying to get through. They can't even see you.

I didn't know where I was going. I didn't really want to know. What hospital, what county. Somebody told me but I must have blocked it out. Denial again. Wherever it was it was miles away and the journey took a long time.

Neil was driving. Wren was in the front passenger-seat getting too much sun. Max sat in the back with me, holding my hand. I fell asleep against his shoulder and when I woke up I had fallen across his lap.

'We're here,' he said, stroking my cheek.

I sat up. My back ached from the twisted position I had been in. 'I'm so sorry. I've been lying all over you.'

But he didn't seem to mind. He leaned forward to see the place, between the two front seats. 'It looks all right,' he said. 'Nice grounds.'

It looked austere to me. Like a posh boarding-school.

'Good job you've got health insurance,' said Neil, pulling up the handbrake, 'or we'd have to sell the house.'

I thought that the word *we* was rather revealing, but Max didn't even blink.

Neil jumped out and opened the door at the back of the Land-Rover, and then he opened the passenger door to fetch Wren.

When I had agreed to being hospitalized, they had recommended that I leave her behind. In Laura's capable hands. I thought, if I'm suffering from this condition they talk about, whatever it is, this psychosis thing, isn't that the most stupid thing they could suggest?

I said I'd sooner kill her. My own baby. I'd sooner kill her myself than let those murderers lay a finger on her. I only agreed to Neil driving because Max didn't have a licence and we couldn't afford a cab. My insurance company wouldn't pay for one.

'I'll carry that,' said Max, taking my suitcase from me.

I took the car-seat from Neil's possessive grasp and unstrapped my chick. She was dopey with sleep, stretching, munching the air.

'You needn't come in,' I said to Neil. He hung back immediately, obediently. 'Max will see to things. Won't you, Max?'

'If that's what you want,' he said.

Had he meant it, about loving me? I was leaning on him in every way that I could. I'd never known need like it. Love, need, need, love. Were they the same, after all?

In the corridor, just past the front door, there was an old woman lying down on the floor, entirely naked. She was flanked by several men and women in white coats, trying to get her up. She was writhing about as they grabbed at her limbs.

'Help me up,' she said. 'I fell down. Help me up. Help me up. I fell down. I fell down. Help me up. I fell down. I fell down. I fell down.'

She repeated herself many more times than this. I know because I watched. I couldn't move for shock. I couldn't believe that this was what I had come to. What she had come to. The stupid indignity of it.

Her inflection was exactly the same with each repetition. Up with *up*, down with *down*. I couldn't help admiring her economic choice of words. They seemed so apt. So pitifully misunderstood.

Max smiled at me, bravely. 'Shall we find Reception?' he suggested. 'I think we've come through the wrong door.'

But we hadn't. Reception was a small window directly opposite us that slid open and shut. A uniformed nurse slid it open and peered out at us. 'Can I help you?'

Max did the talking. I watched the white-coated people carry the old lady along the corridor with great difficulty as she twisted about. She was thin and angular, her ribs more pronounced than her breasts, as though her sex was dripping off her like melting wax.

Then I was led along the same corridor by the nurse, and into a ward that was another corridor with curtains either side, like changing-rooms, hiding more misery from view. More lost souls. My own curtain was blue. The last curtain of all. Blue for the blues. She swept it open proudly to reveal a mattress on a trolley and no window.

Max winced. 'Is this where she's supposed to sleep?'

'It's a hospital, love, not a hotel.'

'Yes I know that,' he said patiently, 'But it's a bloody expensive hospital. The brochure shows private rooms with French doors opening on to gardens. Proper landscaped gardens. This is a cell.'

'If you're not happy, you'll have to take it up with her psychiatrist, I'm afraid. I can't move her myself.'

'And where's the baby supposed to sleep?'

'The baby?' She noticed Wren for the first time. 'Is the baby coming in?'

Max sighed with exasperation. 'Has nobody told you anything?'

'I'm just doing my job,' she said.

'Not very well,' he muttered under his breath.

'New patients never go straight into single rooms. Not since I've been here. Always on the ward first. If you don't like it,' she said, 'no one's twisting your arm.'

With that, she walked away. We watched her go, all the way back down the corridor. There were a few voices calling out from behind their curtains, some in pain, some just talkative, but mostly there was silence.

Max put his arms around us both and kissed the top of my head.

'Please don't go,' I said.

'I can hardly stay, can I?'

'They'll kill you if you go back there on your own.'

'They won't kill me, Anna,' he said, calmly. 'Honestly, they won't. Even if what you say is true. Even if they did try before.'

'They did,' I insisted.

He smiled gently. 'I can't help feeling I'd be the first to know,' he said, 'if someone had tried to kill me. Don't you agree?'

'Do you remember going to meet Laura, at least?'

'Of course I do.'

'And what happened?'

'We had a cup of tea,' he said, coolly.

'And after tea?'

He frowned, as if he wasn't quite sure.

'What happened after tea?' I demanded urgently.

But then another nurse came bustling down the corridor to greet me. She looked more senior. Bigger, bossier, dressed in navy blue.

'I'm Ruth – you must be Anna Stubbs,' she said, closing in. 'And here is your beautiful baby!'

She was southern Irish, a soft, round drawl to her voice that thawed my heart. She put her face up close to Wren's so that Wren could see her features clearly. 'Hello lovely. Aren't you beautiful?' And then she looked up at me as if I was beautiful too and said, 'I'm terribly sorry not to have been here, to greet you when you arrived. I'm afraid our communication has been a tad poor here today. Can I get you a drink, either of you?'

Max was still frowning, trying to remember what happened after tea. 'No thanks,' he said. 'Can you get her a decent room, though? This is a cubicle, it's not even a cell.'

She laughed. 'Horrible, isn't it?' It seemed bearable at once, if she would stay nearby and talk sweetly. 'Shall I have a word with Dr Ferguson, first thing in the morning?'

'Please.'

'What about now?' Max interjected.

'He won't be in again today, I'm afraid.'

'We'll be fine here just for one night,' I said.

'Well I'll leave you to settle in,' Ruth said, 'and say your goodbyes. And then I'll give you a guided tour myself.'

It sounded like an honour, as if she didn't usually give guided tours. She winked at me and then went through an orange curtain further down the corridor and greeted somebody else, her laughter bellowing out into the silence.

'You know,' said Max, 'I can't remember what happened after tea at all. I think I went to sleep.'

I tried to raise one eyebrow, but they both went up.

'All I remember is waking up in bed with a slight headache the next day. Maybe we had some booze.' He paused, thoughtfully. 'Yes, in fact, we did. That's what we did. We drank a superb bottle of Port that Father had always been too mean to touch. It was like a strange kind of celebration. Of his death.'

19

'Well now, guess who's got visitors?' Ruth grinned, swishing back my curtain. 'Your Mum and Dad have come to see you.'

I was horrified and thrilled at once. I didn't want them to see me there, to worry over me. I just wanted them to see my baby and wonder at her.

'They're so excited!' said Ruth.

'How did they know where to find me?'

'Wasn't that young man going to tell them?' She picked up Wren who was gurgling on her back, her legs kicking the air. 'Will you come to them, or will I bring them here?'

'Why couldn't they wait?'

'Now what sort of a question is that? They want to meet their grand-daughter, don't they? They haven't even seen her yet.'

'But why *here*? Why have they come *here*?'

'For the same reason, I should think. A grand-daughter is a grand-daughter, wherever she is. And a daughter is a daughter. They love you, don't they?' She tutted at me.

'I'll come to them,' I said.

They were in what was known as the television room, talking to a paranoid schizophrenic about an invention of his. A flying machine, designed to overcome traffic pollution in our globally warming environment. It sounded good. He was called Michael, and I grew fond of him. He was round and Jewish with shiny brown eyes and a permanent smile across his fleshy face.

'A newcomer in our midst!' he hollered as I followed Ruth into the room.

'What have you been saying, Michael?' Ruth teased. 'These good people look eight times older than they did when I saw them last!'

'I'm trying to get my flying machine flying,' he explained. 'Off the ground. Out into the world. Who are you then?' He beamed at me. I was a little overwhelmed by his energy.

'I'm – '

'You're Anna, aren't you? I knew you were. I've told them you're going to be fine.'

'Now will you stop talking,' Ruth interrupted, 'and help me with the trolley, Michael?'

'Delighted to be of service,' he beamed again, bowing down before her.

'Sorry about that.' She winked. Michael winked too. He'd taken a shine to me. 'I'll shut this door. Give you some peace.'

Well, she gave us silence, at least. I wouldn't call it peace.

Mum stared at me wildly. She looked very lost. Dad stared at his feet. They didn't even look at Wren. Worry seemed to be holding them up like a dense stuffing. Two parked dummies crammed full of fear.

'Hello,' I said.

Mum nodded. Dad looked at his feet.

'This is Wren.'

She nodded again. He didn't even look up.

'What's the matter?' I accused him, irritably.

'It's a wonder you have to ask,' he muttered.

Mum said, 'Can I hold her?'

'I do have to ask,' I said.

'Just think about it,' he barked, looking up at me at last. 'Just bloody think about it.'

'Can I hold her?' Mum repeated.

I passed her my chick. 'Careful of her head,' I said.

'I know that much,' she sniped. 'I know about babies' heads, for goodness sake!'

'Well good,' I said, taken aback. 'I don't know what you know about babies. Newborn babies. I was nine months old before you looked after me.'

She glared at me as if I'd said something unkind. 'Of course I know about babies,' she repeated crossly. 'For goodness sake.'

Wren started crying.

'Fine,' I snapped. 'I'm not a mind-reader.'

'Nor is she,' muttered Dad.

'What's that supposed to mean?'

Mum was trying to comfort Wren by rocking her.

'It's supposed to mean how the bloody hell are we supposed to know you've had the baby if you don't bloody telephone?'

Wren was howling now.

'She doesn't like that,' I said, too sharply.

'All babies like rocking,' Mum argued. 'Rocking is what they like best.'

'Did you hear what I said?' Dad barked at me over Wren's howls and Mum's sniping.

'What? Yes,' I said, 'I heard you, Dad.'

'So?' he asked. 'What's your excuse?'

But I wasn't listening. I was reaching out for my chick. 'Give her to me, would you?' I pleaded.

'No, she's fine.'

'She's not fine,' I said.

'What's your excuse?' insisted Dad, stuck like a record round the same petty grievance.

'She's just getting used to her grandmother,' Mum said.

'*Give her to me!*' I screamed.

They looked at each other as if a bomb had gone off. She gave Wren back instantly, terrified of me. 'All right,' she said. 'Calm down.'

Wren was quiet at once, back with a familiar smell. Familiar family. 'She doesn't know your smell,' I explained. 'You're not genetically coded into her memory.'

'Oh here we go,' said Mum. 'Didn't I tell you, Paul?'

Dad shook his head, as if he were wise or something.

'What did you tell him?'

'I think this whole thing with you,' she said, squaring up to me, 'this whole madness thing, it's all about this. Isn't it?'

'What madness thing? All about what?'

'About your adoption.' She paused, her eyes challenging mine. 'Isn't it?'

'What about my adoption?'

'All this pretending to be mad.'

'I'm not pretending to be mad!'

But she just shook her head, along with Dad, a knowing smile across her face, as if I had done the most predictable thing in the world. 'You don't want to know us any more, do you? Not now you're a *real* mother, do you? That's what it is. I saw it coming, didn't I, Paul?'

'If anyone's mad,' I said, 'It's you.'

I left them sitting there, looking more institutionalized than anyone else in that whole hospital.

Half an hour later, Ruth came to find me. She was less warm than she had been. I guessed that she'd been talking to my parents.

'Will you see Dr Ferguson now?'

'If I must.'

'Well you must,' she confirmed, 'or we may have to section you.'

I followed her obediently down endless corridors, Wren gurgling on my shoulder like a drain. Ruth stopped outside a firmly shut door and knocked very loudly. A scarcely audible grunt came from inside. She ushered me in immediately to meet Dr Ferguson.

'Anna Stubbs for you,' she said.

He was on the telephone, sitting in a leather swivel-chair with his back to us. He spun round, glanced up, nodded to Ruth in acknowledgement, and then bowed his head over copious notes.

She shut the door firmly behind her. Dr Ferguson waved me towards a chair opposite him, where I sat watching him, listening to his conversation. He was a large man, his hair the same colour as mine, rolling back in curiously tight waves from his low forehead. He was very animated, a passionate man who loved his work. You could tell that much at once.

'I don't think so,' he argued.

Brief pause.

'Because I don't think he's depressed enough.'

Pause.

'Another week?'

Pause.

'Five days then. Another five days. If in five days we still think so, then ECT it is.'

Brief pause.

'Good.' He put down the phone. 'Anna. How are you?'

He reached across his desk, his hand outstretched. I tried to shake it but he wanted contact, not formal greetings. He held my hand quite still in his own until I felt uncomfortable. 'How can I help?'

He smiled warmly at me. I wasn't expecting someone so nice. I took my hand away as graciously as I could and said that I didn't know, it wasn't my choice to be there, I didn't think I needed help.

He looked surprised. 'No?'

'Well, not help in the medical sense,' I explained.

'I see.' He nodded. 'Help in what sense, then?'

'I need police protection,' I said. 'That's all.'

He didn't even flinch. 'That's quite a lot,' he said.

I felt that he was possibly taking me seriously. At any rate, he hadn't made up his mind about me before I walked into the room, like the other doctor had.

'Why do you need police protection, do you think?'

'Because someone wants to kill me,' I said.

'I see.' He watched me carefully, his hands in prayer now, the tips of the fingers brushing against his thick lips. 'Who?'

I was glad that he wasn't writing things down or referring to any of his notes. It made me feel more at ease, better able to talk.

'Look, I'm not mad,' I said. 'I know I probably sound

it but I'm not. It's everyone around me who seems to be going mad.'

I kept expecting him to look wary of me, but if he was, he didn't show it.

'Your mother's a little upset,' he said. 'Is that who you mean?'

'Have you spoken to her?'

'She did just pop in briefly,' he admitted. 'At my request.'

'She's mad. She's gone mad. She thinks I don't want to know her any more.'

He nodded, as if he were seeing my point of view. 'Is it your mother who is trying to kill you?' he asked.

'Oh no,' I said. 'I don't think so. Is she?'

He shrugged. 'You tell me.'

'No, I wouldn't say that she was trying to kill me. No. I think she's just a bit thrown, because of the baby.'

'Ah. The baby,' he said. 'How old is she?'

'Oh, days old. That's all. I could probably count the hours.'

He got up and walked round his desk towards her, bending down behind me to see her beautiful face. 'She looks happy, doesn't she? Lucky thing. Not a care in the world.'

'Not yet,' I said.

'So.' He was back in his swivel-chair already, swinging gently. 'Your mother. Thrown. In what way, do you think?'

'Because I was adopted, you see. I think maybe it brings something up for her. Something raw, you know. About not having done it herself. Maybe some feeling of competition, even.'

He nodded. Not in agreement, but just to show that

he was listening. 'So who's trying to kill you, Anna?' he asked, gravely.

'My brother-in-law.'

He leaned forward urgently, as if he believed me. 'Why?'

'Because,' I began, taking a deep breath, 'I'm in his way.'

He leaned back, swivelling in his chair. His hands were praying again.

'When he killed Jack,' I explained, ' – Jack's my husband, the father of my child – When he killed him, he didn't know I was pregnant, you see. He didn't even know we were married. And he certainly didn't know that Max was still alive. So he thought that if he murdered Jack, he would inherit everything. But once Jack was dead, a whole new set of problems emerged. Firstly because I was pregnant, and secondly because Max suddenly turned up out of the blue. So there were two more obstacles in his way.'

'Sorry to interrupt, but who is Max?'

'Max? Max is my friend. He's the middle brother. Not the one who's trying to kill me. At least I don't think he is. Although . . . I've had my doubts.'

Ferguson was looking very confused.

'Neil is the one who's trying to kill me,' I explained.

'Neil,' he repeated. 'Right.'

'And also, I think his wife Laura is in on it all. I think she helps him.'

'Helps him with what?'

'With the murders,' I said.

He leaned forward again, both elbows on the desk, his chin cupped in his hands. 'How many murders are we talking about, here?'

'I don't know for sure. Maybe one. Maybe three. Maybe two attempted murders as well.'

'And who are they, all these murder victims?'

'Firstly there's Clarissa, their mother, who supposedly fell by accident. But in fact she was pushed. Then there's George, their father, who drove off a cliff. And then there's Jack. Who hung himself. And then of course there were the attempted murders, of Max and me.'

Ferguson sat back again restlessly. His eyes were burrowing into mine. 'And what do the police think about it all?' he asked.

'They don't want to know.'

'I see.' He paused thoughtfully. 'You don't think they might have examined the evidence already, and reached their own conclusions about these deaths?'

'Oh yes,' I said. 'They have. But they've got it wrong. Completely wrong.'

'You don't wonder if you might possibly have got it wrong?'

'Of course I've wondered. Of course. It was all guesswork at first. But when you see your own brother-in-law being carried about like a corpse, by the very people you suspect, you wonder a little less and you know a little more. It's too much of a coincidence, don't you think? All those deaths in the space of a year?'

'It does seem unlikely,' he agreed. 'But what strikes me as much more unlikely,' he reasoned on with disappointing simplicity, 'is that any murderer could be so stupid. So obvious.'

'So clever, you mean,' I contradicted him.

There was a long silence while he fiddled with his ear, scrutinizing my open face. 'I'd like to give you some medication, if you don't mind,' he said. He seemed reluctant, twisting his pen round and round in his hands.

'Why?'

'To make you feel a little better. Don't worry. Nothing too strong.'

'But what for?'

'Just – it just sounds like you've had a bumpy ride, Anna.'

'I have. I have had a bumpy ride, but – '

'So let me give you something to make you feel better,' he said.

'What? What's it called?'

'Chlorpromazine, it's called. Know it? Or you may know it as Largactil.'

'What does it do?'

'It's a sedative,' he said. 'Except . . . hang on. I'm not sure I can give it to you if you're breast-feeding.' He flicked through some great medical tome. 'Are you breast-feeding?'

'Yes.'

His finger was trailing down the page. It stopped abruptly while he studied his answer. 'That settles that,' he said, closing the book. 'I can almost certainly give you something that won't interfere with your feeding, but I'm rather inclined to wait.' He hesitated, pen poised in mid-air. 'We'll leave it for a day or two. See how you are then. At least you know you'll be safe here. No one's going to murder you here.'

20

I was moved into a private room the next day. It looked out over a vast lawn, big as a field. A line of beech trees marked out its edge, their elephant-skinned limbs waving leaves like luminous jewels in the sun. Emerald green against a cobalt-blue sky.

Mum came again, just after lunch. She looked like she hadn't slept.

'You're keen,' I said. 'Where's Dad?'

'Oh you know Dad. He's too cross, still.'

Typical, I thought. I'm in a mental hospital with a premature baby and he's feeling sorry for himself.

She sat on my bed like she used to when I was a child, to tell me a story. 'I don't want it to be like this,' she began. She tried to smile, but she was too close to tears. 'I don't want us to fall out over such a wonderful thing. Such a beautiful thing.'

She was looking tenderly at my sleeping chick, her hands twitching in anticipation of her.

'Pick her up, if you like.'

But she already had. She was leaning back a little so that Wren could lie outstretched on her front without scrunching up. She had her round, kind cheek against Wren's downy head. She was sobbing uncontrollably.

I'd never seen her cry before. It looked good for her.

'What did the psychiatrist say?' she asked through her tears.

'Nothing much. Just to give it time.'

'To give what time?'

'Me. Just me. Give me time.'

But she was looking for something more than time in my face, and when she couldn't find it, she turned away. 'Time. Yes,' she said. 'The great healer.'

We were both quiet for a bit.

'Is it very hard for you?' I asked.

'Oh yes,' she smiled bravely. 'It's very hard for me. But there are much worse things in the world. Much harder things to bear, aren't there?'

'I don't know,' I said. 'Why couldn't you have them?'

'I could. I did,' she said. Pause. 'She died.'

A confusing mixture of feelings invaded me. 'Who died, Mum?'

'My baby died.'

But I was your baby, I thought.

'But – how? When?'

'The year before we got you.'

'You had a baby? The year before you got me?'

She nodded.

'A baby girl?'

'Tiny as this.' She stroked Wren's silky head.

'But . . .'

'But she died. Cot-death, they'd call it now. Two months old.'

I could feel all her grief spilling into my own, both of us mixed up in a great flood of it.

'Why didn't you tell me?' I demanded, outrage at the corners of my voice.

She looked at me reproachfully, as if I should know better than to ask.

'But . . . why didn't you have another one? Why did you adopt?'

'It wasn't like that,' she said.

'So what was it like?'

'We didn't go through the formal adoption channels. It wasn't a choice in that way.'

'What do you mean, it wasn't a choice? It can't have been an accident!'

'Oh sweetheart,' she sighed. 'I don't think you should ask. Not just now.'

'I am asking,' I said. 'I'm finally asking you, and you won't tell me.'

She cleared her throat. Looked out of the window at the trees. 'You were given to us,' she said. 'Sort of. You were . . . sort of – a gift.'

'Who from?'

'It's your right to know,' she agreed. 'I know it's your right to know.'

'So who?' I demanded. 'Who didn't want me? Who gave me away?'

'I don't think it was a question of – of not wanting you, Na. I'm sure it wasn't that.'

'Please don't patronize me, Mum. I'm not a child any more. I don't need you to protect my feelings.'

'I'm not patronizing you. Am I? I was always the one who wanted to tell you about it, but you never wanted to know.' She paused reproachfully. 'Your mother had what you've got,' she said.

'What? What have I got?'

'This Purple Psychosis thing. She had it too.'

'I haven't got Purple Psychosis,' I snapped. 'Whatever the fuck that is. I haven't got it. I'm fine.'

She looked as though she was biting her lip so hard that it hurt. 'You're not well,' she said, as if she were the only one brave enough to break the bad news to me.

'So who was she?'

'A friend.'

'Do I know her?'

'No.'

'What was she like?'

'Wonderful. She was wonderful. I couldn't have done it, otherwise.' She pulled an uncertain face at me, as if she might have gone too far.

'It's OK, Mum. I want to know.'

She breathed in and out very loudly.

'How did you meet her?'

'On a bus.'

'A *bus*?'

'We were going to Piccadilly.'

'Actually *on* the bus, or just at the stop?' I asked, as if it mattered.

'On the bus. On the front seat at the top. She sat down next to me and just started talking. Very openly. About her husband. In quite an unsatisfied way. As if she'd been duped into marrying him by the social expectations of the fifties, and now here were the sixties and she was trapped.'

She looked at me for some indication of how I was feeling.

'And?'

'Well I could understand a lot of what she was saying.

Paul and I were going through a very . . . difficult patch. Very . . . bickering. So we got talking.'

'And?'

'It turned out she was pregnant. Which made her feel even more trapped.'

She looked at me nervously, as if she had gone too far even for her, let alone for me.

'I mean trapped with her husband, not with her baby,' she said.

'She could have aborted it,' I said coolly, catching sight of myself in the wardrobe mirror. 'Aborted me.'

Mum looked horrified. 'Aren't you glad she didn't?'

I didn't think it was fair to answer her. But she looked at me in that way of hers that knew anyway, head cocked to one side, seeing into my soul. Her eyes were full of anguish. She shook her head. 'I don't know what's wrong with you,' she said, 'if it's not that psychosis thing. That Purple Psychosis.'

'Puerperal,' I corrected her.

'What?'

But I didn't want to talk about me any more.

'What did you do?' I asked. 'Offer her money?'

'Who?'

'This woman. This mother of mine.'

'Oh no. Not money, Na. It wasn't a business deal. It was just one of those flippant things. She was unhappy because she had a baby, I was unhappy because I didn't. Mine had just died. So I said, if you don't want yours, give it to me.'

She laughed at the memory, her face lighting up like a girl's. 'It was just a joke when I said it. We both knew it was a joke.'

'So how come it happened,' I asked bitterly, 'if it was just a joke?'

She was instantly full of remorse. 'I'm sorry. I'm so sorry. I didn't mean a joke like that. I meant a joke because I didn't think that anyone could ever give a baby away.'

'I know what you meant,' I said, hurting more with every revelation that she made. 'Please stop apologizing.'

'I'm sorry,' she said.

I watched her impatiently, like a child at bedtime still waiting for my story. 'We discovered that we lived very near to each other in Dulwich, and we became great friends, in those ensuing months. We used to meet every Saturday and go out on the town, and we'd meet in the week too, and just talk and talk. There was so much to say, in those days.'

She went all nostalgic.

'And? What actually happened, Mum?'

'Sorry. Yes.' She smiled kindly. 'I think she was quite looking forward to you, in the end. After I'd told her so much about it all, about how wonderful it is to have a baby. But . . .'

'But what?'

'But when you arrived, she just went mad. Really quite mad.'

'Mad in what way?'

'She became very paranoid.'

'About what?'

'About her husband, mainly.'

'What about him?'

'She thought he was plotting to murder her.'

'Why?'

'I don't know why. She thought he was having an affair.

She'd gone right off sex with him, herself. I think she imagined that he wanted to go off with his mistress, and that murder was the only way.'

'And did he?'

'Did he what? Murder her?' she asked.

'Or go off with his mistress?'

'No! No to both.'

I was beginning to feel that I wanted to meet her.

'You still haven't told me how she ended up giving me away.'

'She was admitted to hospital with this thing you've got, and she asked me to look after you while she was there. She said she trusted me. She didn't want her husband looking after you.'

'And? What happened when she came out?'

She didn't answer. She looked at the trees. 'Beautiful day,' she said.

'Mum.'

She looked straight at me and said it again. 'Beautiful day.'

'Tell me.'

'No.'

'I have a right to know. You said so yourself.'

'Not today,' she said. 'That's enough for today.'

She prodded Wren until she stirred, and in no time at all she was all tears again, all open-mouthed with hunger and anger and motherlessness.

'I think she wants you,' said Mum, passing her over to me.

I thought of how I must have wanted my mother too. At that particular moment in time, whenever it was, that she passed me over for ever to the Mum I know now. I must have wanted her so badly. I thought I must have howled my lungs out for days. Maybe even for months. Maybe I never stopped.

But here we were now, and I couldn't imagine wanting any other Mum. She was it. Because of her I knew how to love.

I fed Wren. Her intense blue eyes looked up at me, concentrating hard, as if to make sure I didn't go away again while she was feeding. I don't think she had yet discovered that my breasts were part of me, that I couldn't leave them behind.

'You're not on drugs, are you?' asked Mum.

'No,' I replied. 'So I can't be that mad, can I?'

'Who knows?' she muttered. 'Just as well, with the feeding.'

She looked down at her hands, as if she were reading her palms, as if they could tell her how long I would fight her. I was being so short with her, it hurt. And yet it was still outside me, still something bigger than me that kept pulling us apart. Perhaps it was just a natural thing, another part of the long process of individuation. I knew she understood, forgave me, loved me enough for it, but it hurt all the same. It would hurt until we were through it and out the other side.

'I love you, Mum.'

'Yes,' she smiled. 'I know.' She looked at the trees again. 'Lovely view you've got here.'

'She didn't get out, did she?'

She looked at me. 'Who?'

'Oh come on, Mum.'

'Anna, you mean?'

'Was that her name?'

'Anna, yes. We called you after her.' She looked back at the trees, as if they could give her something she lacked. Courage, perhaps. 'No. She didn't get out. She never got well.'

21

Max was staying in a local pub in Northampton. Which was where the hospital was, apparently, or somewhere near there. He came to visit me shortly after Mum, who was going back to her Sussex bungalow with Dad.

Dad didn't come again. I think that his grief about his own baby was still buried deep down inside him somewhere, and he just couldn't face it. Grief does curious things.

'How are you?' asked Max, pecking my cheek like a brother would.

'I'm fine,' I said, emphatically.

'And Wren?'

He was hovering over her Moses basket, love in his eyes.

'She's fine too.'

He looked at me searchingly. His face was all worried, still.

'I've got to get out of here, Max,' I said. 'Before I start believing all of you. They're very dangerous places, these hospitals.'

'But you've only just got here,' he said.

'Exactly. I've been here a day and everyone is treating me like a full-blown lunatic. It's terrifying. They seem to have stopped expecting sanity from me. Responsible behaviour. Who *wouldn't* go mad?' He looked more worried than ever. 'I don't know,' he said. 'I don't know whether you're mad or not. I don't know you well enough.'

'You're my only hope,' I pleaded. 'You're the only one who even vaguely shares some of my suspicions. You've got to tell them.'

'But they're two different things,' he said, frowning hard. He was struggling to be fair, like a good judge. 'Our suspicions and your mental health. They're separate issues.'

'I'm as mentally healthy as you, Max. Our suspicions are why I'm here.'

'*Your* suspicions, not ours, not the ones we've shared.'

'You cheat,' I said. It felt like betrayal, however well-intentioned he was.

'I'm not cheating, Anna, I'm just trying to get at the truth. I'm trying to be impartial.' He looked at me for some forgiveness. It was unforthcoming.

'Your suspicions about Neil and Laura seem very far-fetched, even to me. I can't pretend otherwise. It wouldn't be fair, least of all to you. I mean, all this stuff about seeing me dead. It's . . . mad.'

'You don't remember what happened after the port,' I reminded him coldly.

'You're right, I don't. But the more I think about it, the more likely all those suicides seem. I have a very dark family history, you know.'

'How dark?'

But he did that same thing Mum had done, of looking out at the trees. 'Very majestic, those beeches, aren't they?'

'I know that George used to beat you all,' I challenged him. 'But – I know it's awful to be beaten, I'm not belittling it, but it's quite common, isn't it? It's not so unusual. It's no reason to top yourself.'

'It's curious, isn't it,' he said, deflecting stubbornly, 'how beautiful a place can be, and yet it can still house such misery. A place like this. A place like Barkwood. Beauty is nothing, is it, really? Without love.'

'Lots of people are beaten by their parents – do they all kill themselves? Aren't they more likely to kill someone else? Violence breeds violence.'

'I guess there must be different kinds of violence,' he said. 'There are parents who lash out, parents who punish, and there are sadists.'

'And George was what? A sadist?'

'Just a little.'

'What did he do that was so sadistic?'

He furrowed his smooth brow. 'Think about Wren,' he said. 'How much you love her. The lengths you'd go to, to protect her from harm.' I'd kill. 'Father was the opposite. It was as if he *sought* harm, relished it, enjoyed its impact on us. I don't know what it was about him. I keep trying to understand, I keep puzzling over his choices – how he could have made them, how different they were from mine.'

'And?'

'I don't get anywhere. Not really. The only reason I can come up with is that he couldn't ever stand the thought of other children getting something he never had himself – even if it was his own children. You know how kids are when things are unfair, how vicious they become towards each other. It was that kind of viciousness, only he was a grown man, so it was infinitely more dangerous.'

'What kind of viciousness, though?'

'Sometimes it was random – well, no, it was always random, so in that sense it *was* like a frustrated parent. You could never predict when it would come. Sometimes he'd be in a rage and we'd all just hide, but more often it was too subtle to predict. He'd do this fake nice thing, warm and friendly and fatherly, luring you towards him, and you always knew not to trust it but you wanted to even so, every time, you wanted to believe that really he loved you and finally he'd show you he did, and he'd say sorry for the last time he snapped at you, which was usually the last time he even spoke to you at all, and then just when you got close enough to him, he'd hit you. Really hard. You'd see his enormous hand slice through the air towards your face. And then he'd laugh, as if it was really funny. And then he'd be nice again, almost cuddle you, prod your tummy playfully, tickle you until you laughed, and then he'd wind you. A real punch in the gut. And then he'd take off his belt or grab something else to hand and swipe your backside. It was usually Jack he did first. Jack was always the most keen for the love. And then when he'd amused himself sufficiently with this bizarre combination of laughter and violence, he'd lock him in the cellar, and make us all taunt him on the other side of the door.'

'I didn't know there was a cellar at Barkwood.'

'There's a huge cellar. It stretches the length of the house.'

'Did he only lock Jack in it?'

'Mostly Jack, but all of us on different occasions. He very rarely persecuted us all at the same time. It wasn't to his advantage. He preferred to have us side with him against his victim, whoever that was on any given day. It was divide and rule, basically. It worked immaculately. We ended up not trusting each other at all. We betrayed each other all the time, just to keep him sweet, just to avoid being his target ourselves. We'd persecute each other the way he did. It never changed, that. You can see for yourself how little we had to do with each other in adulthood.'

'Why did he pick on Jack so much?'

'He was the oldest. He stood up to him the most. It was like a power struggle, almost. He seemed to perceive Jack as quite threatening, as if he was his equal and not a small weak boy at all. Maybe it was some history Father had with his younger brother, maybe that's what he was still acting out.'

He bowed his head over Wren's little Moses basket, and then looked up at me. 'But in fact, the cellar thing, he got a taste for that.'

'What do you mean, a taste for it?'

'He put us all down there, in the end. It became our living quarters. The scary thing then was being invited *out* of the cellar!' He laughed, as if it really was a funny twist in a half-amusing little tale. 'Then you really knew what you were in for!'

'You lived in the cellar?' I asked, trying to keep up.

'Yes. I mean, it sounds awful now, but it wasn't that bad. It didn't seem that bad. A bit damp, cold. But it was like we had our own private den where we felt safe. We could relax a bit, get into some game, and really play quite well together. And then we'd hear his footsteps approach overhead and the fun would end. That feeling of dread would kick in. We'd just sit there in silence waiting for the lock to turn.'

'Did you sleep there too?'

'Oh no. It was just a sort of daytime place.'

'But he'd lock you in?'

'We had a sort of loo, a bucket and stuff. It wasn't so bad.'

'And he'd call one of you out to beat you?'

'He'd usually invent some ridiculous reason. Which we'd try to understand, so that we could avoid repeating it and thus avoid another beating, but it didn't work like that. The reasons were never consistent. I remember once he actually threw Jack down the stairs after he'd beaten him. He came crashing down like a sort of heavy doll. When I think about that now, he could've killed him. Broken his fucking neck. We thought he had, at first. It was almost as if that was what he was trying to do, as if he was beating us just to edge of death, sometimes. Especially Jack. Even when he was beating me or Neil, it was still like a way to get at Jack.'

'Oh Max,' I said. Tears were streaming down my face. 'I didn't know.'

He put an arm around me. 'It's OK. It's not your fault,' he said. 'If Jack didn't tell you, it's not your fault.'

'But he – he did, in a way.'

'He didn't though, did he? Not really, at all.'

'Not in detail, like you have, but he did sort of tell me, he sort of implied it, it was always there, lurking behind what he said.'

'But even if he did, Anna, even if he'd given you a blow-by-blow account, you can't blame yourself if he took his own life.'

'But I could've – I could've helped him, I could've – loved him more. I could've – saved him.'

'He didn't want saving. Did he, Anna?' He was almost shaking me. 'Did he?'

'Didn't he?'

'If he'd wanted saving, he would've asked for it. He would've asked.'

'Maybe he did. Maybe he did ask. Maybe I just didn't hear.'

'Stop it,' he said, sharply. 'Stop doing this.'

'I'm not doing anything. I'm just trying to – '

'If you failed him,' he pleaded, 'what did I do?' His face was tortured with remorse.

I thought, not you too. Don't you go too. I put my arms around him. I tried to kiss the pain away from his face, but it wasn't going anywhere, and I thought that maybe that was good, it shouldn't go, it should stay and be felt, so that he could move on, move through it and out the other side.

We stayed like that for a long time. Just holding on. Until Wren woke up, sensing something. The way babies do.

22

I was there another week without medication. Max came every day, just to reassure me that no one had killed him. The rest of the time I spent talking to Michael. I found him alarmingly interesting. I tried not to show this in public, in case it counted against me, but his imagination inspired me so much, I almost preferred it to sanity.

After a week, Ferguson summoned me back into his office. 'I've spoken to Max,' he said. 'Your brother-in-law.'

'Yes, I know who Max is.' I didn't like the sound of brother-in-law. 'What did you speak to him about?'

'About you. Primarily.'

'What about me? What did he say?'

'Some fairly horrifying things.'

'About me?' I asked, aghast.

'No. Good Lord, no. About his family.'

'So what did he say about me?'

Ferguson swivelled to and fro in his chair, looking at me thoughtfully. 'That he thought you were quite sane. That he'd shared a lot of your misgivings about these various deaths himself, until quite recently. That they were very legitimate speculations, given the circumstances.'

I breathed a sigh of relief.

'I don't know why he didn't say so before. Do you?'

I shrugged. 'I think he was just – going along with

medical opinion,' I suggested. 'It's very easily done, isn't it? It sounds as if my mother was a victim of that.'

'Your mother?'

'My real mother, I mean.'

'Possibly,' he said, 'although I'd be breaking rank even to concede that much.' He narrowed his eyes at me. 'Anyway, he doesn't seem to think you should stay here, this brother-in-law of yours.'

'Do you agree with him?'

'I think I do. Do you?'

'Please,' I begged. 'Please let me go.'

He smiled kindly. 'It's not a prison here, Anna. You can go when you like. I certainly won't section you, if you want to discharge yourself.'

I almost ran down the corridor, Wren welded on to my front as if she were part of me, a growth like a shoot. I called Max and left a message asking him to hire a car that afternoon. I felt fit enough to manage the drive. I threw everything I had into my suitcase and parked it by the door. Then I changed Wren's nappy before it exploded. And finally, I went to find Michael. To say goodbye.

He was in the corridor near reception, talking to a thin old lady who wore baggy jeans with an elasticated waist.

'Michael, I have to go.'

'Anna, Anna!' he beamed. 'Do you know Anna?'

'Hello.' I smiled at his introduction of me.

She smiled too, but it was more like a twitch than a smile, as if she were nervous of me. She looked at Wren, and then looked frantically everywhere else, as if she had come into a magnetic field from the wrong end.

I recognized her as the woman I had seen on my first day there. The naked old lady who had called out for help from the floor.

'She's been here for as long as you've been alive,' he said.

I thought of my real mother, of how the same could be said of her, wherever she was locked away. I thought I might try and find her one day.

'I'm discharging myself,' I said.

The old lady frowned uncertainly. Thin lines engraved themselves across her forehead. The concept seemed alien to her.

'Are you going to fly, or are you going to walk?' asked Michael.

'Don't be silly, Michael,' she said.

Her voice was clear and precise and middle-class. I thought for a wild fleeting moment that it might be her, that I need look no further; fate had put my mother in my very path.

'I think we'll probably drive,' I said, stealing a good look at her as I smiled her way.

I thought that I wasn't ready to meet my mother yet, even if this was her now smiling back at me nervously, squinting her small brown eyes into sharp tight pinheads at me.

'You're very bold,' she said.

'Ferguson thinks it's fine,' I retorted.

I suppose there was a little part of me that wanted to urge them towards the same freedom of self-responsibility.

Michael said, 'Ferguson is a god who escaped the flames of Mars by flying away.' Which was a fairly predictable response. He always said something completely irrelevant when he didn't fancy facing up to a thing, or arguing it through.

'So anyway,' I said, 'I wanted to say goodbye.'

'Goodbye, Anna,' he said indifferently. 'Say goodbye to Anna, Lily.'

'Goodbye, Anna,' said Lily.

'Hello Lily,' I said, my voice faltering, like a novice on a tightrope. My heart was thudding like someone thumping on a door, calling out for freedom at last.

I took her cold, thin, resisting hand in mine. It was soft as a baby's, as if it hadn't touched very much, as if it didn't want to touch now, as if it were too late now, for touching things. She snatched it sharply away.

'I love my home,' she said. 'This is my home. I love my home.'

This could be my mother, I thought. And I don't know if I love her or not.

'I told them, Anna, didn't I?' Michael exclaimed. 'Freedom is a house.'

But I was looking at Lily as her eyes flitted about, unsettling themselves on anything but me.

'I told them, didn't I?' repeated Michael angrily.

'You did, you told them,' I appeased him, uncertain of what he meant.

And then Lily reached out to touch Wren. 'I wish I'd had children,' she said, her baby-soft hand cupping the back of Wren's head.

It felt cruel. A deliberate rebuff. As if she really was my mother and knew she was, too, and was disowning me outright, denying me to my face.

'I must go,' I said, confused by my own inventiveness. 'Max is hiring a car. I mustn't be late.'

'Why are you driving? Fly!'

He was very emphatic about it. I had to explain that I didn't have a plane. 'I'll come and visit you,' I said.

I think I meant Lily more than Michael, but he beamed enthusiastically. 'Fly here,' he said.

'I will if I can,' I agreed.

I kept looking back at her over my shoulder as I walked away. She watched me too, very steadily, no more flitting eyes. But Michael had forgotten me already. He had his back to me and was talking to her vigorously while she studied me. All the way. Right up to the moment I turned the corner.

Max was waiting for me outside my door. 'They're holding a car for us,' he said.

I couldn't get Lily out of my head. She moved in and stayed there. Or was it my heart? I was never sure which was which. Some part of me, anyway. Somewhere inside me that was forever hers.

The drive back down to Devon was long and slow. We had to stop every hour or so to feed Wren or change her or just to cuddle her. Max sat on the back seat with her and tried to make her laugh. Which made me think of Jack.

'There was a photograph,' I told him at last. 'A photograph that Jack developed, but it was under-exposed.'

Wren was asleep. He leaned forward, his chin at my shoulder. 'So?'

'It was around the time of George's death.'

'Is it relevant? A clue, or something?'

'I think it might be.'

'What was the photograph?'

'Well that's what I'm saying. I don't know. It was under-exposed.' I turned off the motorway for the M25.

'I fail to see the significance,' he said.

'So did I, at the time. It may still have no significance,' I conceded. 'All I do know is that he was very very preoccupied with it. So much so that he hardly took it in when I told him I was pregnant.'

I could feel the warmth of Max's breath against my neck. 'Sorry to be ignorant,' he said, 'but what does under-exposed mean, exactly?'

'Too dark,' I said. 'Not enough light.'

He laughed dryly. 'Oh well,' he grinned, 'that's bound to be a clue!'

'I keep wondering whether . . . if I found the photograph somewhere, whether I'd be able to make out what it was – however vaguely.'

'Who knows?' he shrugged.

'Or I could do a lighter print of it, if I could find the neg.'

'Don't miss the turning,' he said.

At tea-time we stopped for something to eat, at a Little Chef. I had a Danish Pastry. Max had a burger and chips. Wren snored loudly in her car-seat.

'What was the secret, Max?'

'The secret?'

'The reason you went away. Your mother's letter. The reason you came back.'

He looked down at his plate. Fiddled with his chips.

'You must tell me. It's not fair if you don't.'

He took a bite out of his burger. I watched him chew. Waited for him to finish his mouthful.

'She had a lover, didn't she?'

'Who told you that?'

'Oh I knew *that* much when I was a teenager.'

'Well I don't know how,' he said, amazed. 'No one else did.'

'Is that the secret then?'

He looked down at his plate again. Shook his head. 'Not all of it. No.'

'I didn't think so.'

He exhaled loudly, blowing at the fringe of his hair. 'How did you know about her lover?' he asked.

'I overheard a conversation between your parents,' I said. 'About you. Blackmailing them.'

He laughed. A dull, blunt laugh.

'So what's the rest of the secret? The part of it that brought you back after twenty years.'

'It's to do with . . .' His voice trailed off.

'Oh come on, Max. Please.'

'It's to do with Neil.'

I tried to guess, but he didn't give me time.

'To do with Neil's parentage,' he explained.

'George isn't his real father,' I realized immediately.

He nodded.

'The lover is his real father.'

He nodded again.

'Good God.' I paused. My real mother smiled anxiously at me out of my fantasy.

'How does anyone know that sort of thing for sure?'

'You've only got to look at Neil, really,' said Max. Which was true. He didn't look anything like either of his parents, the way the other two did. I wondered if I looked like my real mother at all.

'Does he look like his real father then?'

'The spitting image,' said Max.

I thought that I could see his father in my mind's eye, as if I knew him, but his exact features eluded me.

'It's curious how important parentage is. You wouldn't think so, in this day and age, with adoption and surrogacy and IVF. But I bet that, to George, it mattered more than anything.'

Max laughed. A laugh of recognition. 'He was a Victorian, my father. Through and through. A fucking self-righteous Victorian.'

'Were they lovers for a long time?'

'Oh, for years. They went on for years.'

'It must have been painful for George,' I conceded.

'He didn't know. He thought it was just a fling.' Max pushed his plate to one side. 'And even if he did know, he deserved every ounce of pain he ever felt, that man. He deserved to suffer more than anyone.'

Jack again. Always there. In everything he said or did.

'How did *you* know about the affair?'

'I found a letter from her.'

'To her lover?'

'To her lover.'

'What did it say?'

'It said a great deal about Neil. I didn't realize why, at all, but when she caught me, she assumed that I did. She begged me – ' he winced at the memory, 'she begged me on her hands and knees not to tell Father that Neil wasn't his son. I was such an opportunist, Anna. You'd have hated me then.' He looked for something in my expression that said otherwise.

'I loved you then,' I said. 'As you well know.'

'But do you love me now?' It was almost involuntary, a reflex question, like a ball bouncing back.

'I don't know, Max.'

Which wasn't true. I did know. But it could wait. It had waited twenty years, after all.

'So did you tell George?' I persevered.

He shook his head. 'I promised her that I wouldn't say anything about Neil, but that I would tell Father about her lover if she didn't give me enough money and means to leave home.'

'Which you did. You told him about her lover. Didn't you?'

'Yes, I did. Because she couldn't give me any money without Father's consent. But I didn't say who it was. I didn't name him. I didn't go that far, despite enormous pressure from him.'

'And did you tell him about Neil?'

He shook his head again. 'Even I wasn't that low. I think he would have killed him, if I had.'

'So Neil doesn't know?' I asked.

He shrugged. 'I have a feeling he does. But I don't know how.'

We both went quiet for a bit. Wren's little mouth was sucking at the air for milk that wasn't there.

'You know what I think?' I said. 'I think that Clarissa wrote to you to say that George had found out. Or that Neil had found out. Or that both of them had found out.'

He eyed me warily. 'Why do you say that?'

'Because it's true, isn't it? She wrote to say, "Help me,

Max. Come home and deny it to them. You're my only hope. Come home before they kill me." But you didn't come home, did you? Not until it was too late. Until she was dead. Until one or other of them had murdered her for her little misdemeanour.'

He was cringing with shame, its hot red blood seeping across his face.

'Am I right?'

He hung his head. 'You know you're right. Of course you're right,' he admitted, defeat riddling his voice. 'Father had found out about Neil, yes. And about the fact that the affair had lasted almost as long as their marriage had.'

'Why didn't you tell me?'

He shook his head. 'I'm sorry. I've been so – unsure.'

'Of what?'

He blew out like a full-up balloon. 'Of everyone. You. Neil. Jack. Drake. Everyone. You have to admit, it's all been fairly baffling. And once that seed of doubt is there, it plants itself everywhere.'

I knew what he meant.

'As soon as I heard about her death, I felt suspicious,' he said. 'In fact I felt more than suspicious. I *knew*. But frankly, I didn't care very much . . . Is that terrible? It feels terrible. It feels like a truly shocking thing to say.'

'It is. But if it's true, it's true. Nobody cared about her, it seems. Not even Jack.'

'She was a lousy mother, Anna. Cold. Sadistic. Emotionally very cruel. It was hard to respect her, especially the way Father used to treat her. But then when Father died, and then Jack, I had to come and see for myself. Even when I stopped suspecting you, Anna, I still felt caught in the middle.'

'In the middle of what?'

'In the middle of you and Neil. A conflict of loyalties. An increasing loyalty to you. I don't know. I can't excuse it,' he said. 'But I so wanted to make up for – make up for being – ' he swallowed hard, 'for being so useless to Neil, to both of them, to Neil and Jack, for leaving them in the lurch like I did. I so wanted to believe he was innocent. Or that even if he wasn't, I could forgive him. That I could understand.'

'You could forgive him for murder?'

'For her murder, yes. And certainly for his. But – '

'And for Jack's? Could you forgive him for Jack's?'

'Hold on,' he said, 'we don't even know if he murdered *anyone* yet.'

'But if he did?' I shouted. 'Could you forgive him for Jack's?'

He reached across the table for my hand. I snatched it away.

'Oh Anna,' he said. 'Don't do this to yourself. Jack killed himself. Whatever else went on there, I believe that Jack had very good reason to kill himself. I don't know why he chose that particular moment to do it, but I think that he did it. I think that he did it for one of three reasons, or maybe for all three of them.'

I didn't want to know. I was still trying so hard to deny it. I knew that his misery was more than I could hope to bear. I didn't want it described in any more detail.

'The first reason . . . Anna, are you listening?'

'Yes. I'm listening.'

'The first reason is that he was terrified of being a father himself.' He paused for an uncomfortably long time, searching my face. 'I can understand that. I've felt it myself.'

'He would have been a perfect father,' I said. 'Spectacular.'

'The second reason is that he, too, suspected Neil of killing Father, which confirmed his worst fears about the nature of violence, how it gets handed down. And the third reason was that he guessed, along with the rest of us, that Mother was pushed. By a member of his own family. His brother or his father.'

'It's all very hypothetical, this,' I said.

'No it's not. It's all very probable.'

He wouldn't let me off the hook. He kept pulling me in until my whole body hurt. 'You've got to face up to it, Anna. Jack almost certainly killed himself. There's only so much darkness that one soul can withstand.'

Wren woke up and cried instead of me, inconsolable sobs, as if she had woken to an empty world, nobody alive in it but her.

'I don't know how you know so much and I don't,' I said, unstrapping her.

'I'll tell you, one day.' He leaned across the table. Brushed my cheek. 'You look so – '

'We must go,' I interrupted. 'There's a long way to travel yet.'

'Literally, or metaphorically?' asked Max, eating my discarded pastry.

'Both.'

He paid. I went back to the car to feed Wren. As I

walked out into the car-park it started to rain, a light relieving shower, opening out smells. The smell of lost time. Lost love. Loss. The smell of grass and hot tarmac and damp, musty earth.

23

It was dark by the time we got back. Darker still as we turned into the drive. There were lights on in the house. One in the master bedroom which flooded the lawn at the side. Another on the upstairs landing, pouring over the forecourt.

'Somebody's here,' whispered Max. 'Cut the engine.'

I did.

'And the headlights. Quick.'

We sat invisibly beneath the horse-chestnut trees, waiting to be found. The moon was half-full and half-obscure, its cold glimmer shimmering through the leaves. Neil came to the window of the upstairs landing. He pressed his face right up against it so that his nose went flat, hands either side of his eyes to keep out the light. Then he said something over his shoulder and the light went out, but we could still see him quite clearly, standing there in his blue pyjamas, trying to see. Laura joined him. Then both of them moved away. Seconds later the front door swung open and Neil ran out towards us with a gun of some kind, the sort you would use to kill a bird. When he was only a few feet away, he stood still and took aim.

It was a moment that seemed to stretch beyond time, nobody moving at all. And then he let the gun fall slowly away from him until it hung idly in one hand at his side. He leaned forward, squinting into the car.

'What are *you* doing here?'

'It's my home,' I said. 'I've come home.'

He looked pained by my statement. 'So why don't you drive on up?' he asked, waving us through with his gun.

He turned his back on us and went on up himself, his head bowed low.

As soon as we were inside the house it became apparent that they had actually moved in. It felt inhabited, the way it used to feel.

Laura came downstairs, tying up her dressing-gown. 'Anna! What a surprise!'

I couldn't smile the way she could, even on a good day, never mind managing it through adversity.

'How *are* you?'

'I'm fine,' I said. 'I was always fine.'

She gave me a placatory nod. 'And how's the little one?'

'Not so little any more.'

There was an awkward silence. We all seemed to be sizing each other up.

'How come you're both here?' asked Max.

'We – we – sort of – were in the habit of it,' Neil spluttered out.

'Since when?'

'Since – since Anna first got ill.'

Max raised one eyebrow. 'But she wasn't ill, was she? Not really. You knew that.'

Laura furrowed her brow. 'Wasn't she?' she asked.

'Are you sleeping in the main bedroom?' Max ploughed on. 'Mother and Father's old room?'

'Just for the time being,' said Neil.

Max threw open the living-room door, which adjoined the hall. He switched on the overhead light there and looked about him, sniffing the air. 'Goodness me,' he said. 'It's very spick and span in here. Very homely and lived in and . . . different.'

Neil glanced at Laura.

'I wanted to get it all nice for you,' she said to me, improbably.

'Were you expecting me, then?'

Her smile was fading fast. 'Not exactly.'

'You know,' said Max, 'what's puzzling me, is how you had the presumption to move in like this, when not only is it not your house, but it's not even *nearly* your house.'

'It *is* my house,' Neil said suddenly, without meaning to, as surprised as we were by the assertion.

Max looked at him coldly. 'Say that again.'

'Nothing.'

'It didn't sound like nothing to me.'

'Father promised me this house,' he muttered under his breath.

Up went Max's eyebrow. 'That's news to me.'

'Well you weren't here, were you?' he spat. 'Everything's news to you, you fucking little runaway.'

I could see every muscle in Max's body tense. 'When did he promise you this house?'

'For as long as I can remember. He always talked about it, about when I would live here, about what a true, loyal son I was, how he'd leave it to me, how he'd leave everything to me.'

Max smiled, almost kindly.

'He never really let you go, did he? That bullying father

of ours. He never kicked you out of the nest, not until the very end. And now you don't know how the fuck to fly.'

'Fuck you,' spat Neil. 'You could've saved me the trouble if you'd stopped to think.'

'What trouble?'

'The trouble of fucking serving him like some slave all my life. Fucking waiting on them hand and fucking foot.'

Laura had her hands over her ears, as if she had heard it all too many times before, as if it were wearing her down, as if she had to protect herself from it somehow, or die.

'You could've fucking told me, Max. You could've told me when I was just a boy. When I had my whole life ahead. Instead of fucking off, watching your own fucking back.'

He was small, Neil. Five foot nine at most. But as he shouted at Max, he seemed to grow enormous. 'Now I've got nothing,' he said. 'I've got fuck-all to show for it. Fucking fuck-all.'

Max looked at me, his eyebrow doing its thing. 'Neil,' he said, 'I'm really sorry. I let you down badly.'

Neil shrank immediately, almost to half his normal size.

'I should have told you, you're right. More than that, I should've told somebody out there, when I was free, what that man was doing to us. He should've been stopped.'

Neil shrugged vaguely, as if he weren't quite sure what Max meant.

'But it takes so long for the penny to drop. It was years

before I realized how brutal father was, how abnormal it was to be beaten like that. To be locked in a cellar for days on end; not even fed, sometimes; not loved, never *loved* at all. Even Mother never really had anything to give, did she? Fucking empty-handed, both of them.'

Neil was frowning with concentration, trying to grasp what Max was getting at. 'Brutal?' he queried. 'What do you mean? Abnormal what? What was abnormal?'

Max stared at Neil in disbelief. 'Do you even have to ask?'

'I mean, no. Of course. It's a horrible thing to do. Lock someone in a cellar.' He was nodding too vigorously in agreement. Laura had taken her hands away from her ears. She was listening attentively, as if the argument held special significance for her.

'But those beatings, Neil,' Max insisted. 'What about those bloody beatings we had? Don't they seem brutal to you?'

Neil scratched his head. 'Well he didn't often beat me, you see. Not often. It was mainly Jack, wasn't it? Or you. But mainly Jack.'

'Oh so that was OK, was it, Neil? If it was mainly Jack, it didn't really count.' Max put his hand on my arm, silencing me.

'I don't see what's so terrible', Laura piped up, 'about spanking a child who misbehaves. Which obviously Jack did.'

Max looked at her. 'Don't you?'

'Well not really, in all honesty. Neil beats me sometimes, you know, if I overstep the mark. But only when I really deserve it.'

A deathly hush.

'But Laura,' I stumbled, 'you told me about George beating Clarissa and the boys as if it shocked you to the core!'

A cloud passed over Neil's face, so dark that you could hardly see him.

Laura went very quiet, glancing nervously at Neil.

'You beat your wife?' asked Max.

'Only when she provokes me,' he said, glaring at her, as if here was an example of precisely that.

'I never mean to,' she explained, the emotion rising in her voice. 'But I can't seem to get it right. I must be terribly stupid. I always seem to say something insensitive just at the worst time.'

'Don't you just,' he muttered under his breath.

'But that's not an excuse,' I said. 'He doesn't have the right to hit you, Laura, however insensitive you are.'

'It's not like that,' she said.

'What is it like then?'

Silence.

'Laura? What is it like?' I insisted. 'Because I don't understand. How can you object to George's violence and not to Neil's?'

'You don't understand, you're right,' she said.

'So explain it to me.'

'You don't know how unhappy he is. It's not violence as such, it's not like that. He just gets upset. He's always sorry afterwards.'

'Am I allowed to speak?' asked Neil.

Max said, 'I don't think you are. I don't want to hear from you. Does anybody else?'

Laura's unerasable smile was just a line across her face, so tight that you could cut yourself on it. She wasn't wearing make-up, for once, so that you could almost see who she was.

Neil moved his hand up to his forehead to ease the tension there. Laura flinched. Her face trembled like a quivering leaf betraying an impending storm, feeling its air long before it breaks. Involuntary spasms pulled at her face. Tears coursed down her cheeks.

Max was staring at Neil, who saw nothing but Laura's betrayal waving in front of him, red rag to a bull. His nostrils seemed visibly to flare. His eyes became uninhabited, a thick fixed glaze to them, almost robotic, seeing ahead one simple task to execute, one precise order to obey. His mouth was a tight clamp, locking in his vitriol.

Max said, 'I'd feel much happier, Neil, if you stayed at your own place tonight.'

'Don't worry,' he replied with glacial courtesy, 'I fully intend to.'

He moved towards the door, grabbing Laura's arm and directing her out ahead of him. He seemed unaware of his inherent aggression, as though only an actual beating would count against him in our eyes.

'Laura can stay,' said Max.

She looked round at him, terror in her eyes. 'I . . .'

'She'll be fine with me,' Neil said. 'Won't you, my dear? I'm not going to beat her, don't worry.' He pushed her forward.

Max stood in front of them both, blocking their way. 'I would rather she stayed,' he said. 'You go home on your own. That's not a problem, is it?'

Neil's eyes went as thin as arrow slits. 'You'll regret this,' he said, glaring at us one by one. And then he left.

I looked at Wren, sitting in her car-seat at my feet. She

was wide awake, watching, as if she could feel it all, understand it all, know not to cry. Laura sat on the bottom step of the staircase and buried her head in her hands. I sat down next to her, put my hand on her shoulder. Wren watched us, wondering if she might be allowed to cry now too, if Laura was crying.

'It's all right,' I said.

'It's not. You shouldn't have done that. It just makes everything worse.'

Max raised an eyebrow, shook his head with incomprehension. 'You're participating,' he said. 'For as long as you talk like that, you play an active part in his violence.' He paused. 'Shall I make some tea?'

I suggested something stronger. He found a bottle of malt whisky that I had brought down from London. Not that I liked it much, but it was Jack's and he loved it and I couldn't throw it away.

24

The tapping again. I'd forgotten about it.

It was a hot sticky night. I hadn't slept at all. My mind had been beating a path like a drum, round and round Barkwood House. Their hideous childhood there. Neil's violence. Jack's suicide. Whether or not I believed it. And if I did, how angry I felt. How betrayed. How unforgiving of him. Of them. Of all of them. And then, suddenly, the tapping started again.

I tried to see the time without turning on the light. I had to open the shutters to borrow the moon, half-full as it was. Or half-empty, if that's how you see things. I think I saw it as both.

Half past two.

I looked out over the lawn towards the church, wondering if Max was at those graves again, and if he was, why. But I couldn't see anything except the new headstones, like two white teeth gnawing their way into the night. I decided to take a look. Wren was fast asleep in my bed and I tried not to wake her as I opened the door. For the first time since I'd been there, I hadn't locked it. I tiptoed quietly out on to the landing, where I paused to listen again.

Tap tap tap. Like a woodpecker.

Max had left his door ajar. I pushed it open and called out to him in a loud whisper. 'Max!'

He turned over restlessly and went straight back to sleep.

'Max!' I whispered again.

'Eh?' He sat bolt upright, as if a part of him had been wide awake all night.

'Shhh.'

'Anna! What are you – '

'Shhh. Listen.'

'What?' He listened.

'Can you hear it?'

He nodded. He turned his head to one side to hear it better still.

'What the fuck is it?' he asked.

'I don't know. I've heard it before. Is it Neil?'

'I expect so. Up to no good.'

He climbed out of bed, realized that he was completely naked and climbed back in again. 'Since you don't know if you love me,' he said, 'can you pass me that pile of clothes?' He wriggled under the sheets, trying to dress himself. 'Most women would avert their gaze, wouldn't they?' he said. 'You must love me, really.'

I smiled, wondering how I would ever tell him. He climbed out of bed as soon as his shorts were on, and dived into a T-shirt.

'When did you hear it before?'

'Every night. I've heard it every night since I've been here.'

'Why didn't you say?'

'Because I thought it might be you. I suspected you just as much as you suspected me.'

'Fair enough,' he whispered. 'Where's Wren?'

'Asleep.'

'Do you want to stay with her, or come with me?'

'Neither,' I said. 'Both.'

'Come on then. Come with me. I feel like I need you.'

He led the way, his bare feet making no sound.

'I know every creaking floorboard of this house,' he whispered. 'I remember them all. Like a map in my mind.'

I tried to tread where he trod, but invariably I got it wrong and betrayed my exact whereabouts effortlessly. Every time the tapping stopped, we stopped too. Then it would start again and off we would go.

'Is Laura in bed, do you know?' he asked.

'I didn't check.'

'What's the betting she turns out to be a psychopath?'

I think it was meant to be a joke. I didn't find it funny at all. 'Please, Max.'

'All eventualities,' he whispered. 'Be prepared.'

We were just in the hall, standing still again, waiting for the tapping to resume, when Max went very strange. It was so quiet that I could hear him breathe. In and out. Calm and regular. But when the tapping started again he breathed in very sharply and didn't move at all. I almost collided with him where he stood, stock-still in front of me. His face was turned back towards me so that I could see the terror spread over it like a rash. He closed his eyes very tightly and exhaled, as if he were trying to blow away a new and uncontainable fear.

'What is it?' I asked.

He didn't answer.

'Max? What is it? Say.'

But he was still listening, as if he couldn't believe it, and then as if he could believe it, he had to believe it, because it was true. 'It's the cellar,' he whispered. 'It's coming from the cellar.'

He looked so terrified that it somehow reinforced me, as if he were a child of mine to protect. But fear is contagious too, and his infected me. Of course, I thought. It's coming from the cellar. Of course.

'Which way is the cellar?' I asked as calmly as I could.

He pointed in the direction of the kitchen, away from the hall towards the back of the house. Instantly, I remembered my second morning there, standing in the kitchen on my own, and yet feeling the strange, unaccountable presence of somebody else in the room.

'Are you coming or do you want to stay here?'

'I'm coming,' he whispered. 'Just hang on.'

He was trying to snap out of himself. Fear was tying him in knots like a strait-jacket. He seemed almost emasculated by my show of boldness. But I had his strength to protect me. And I didn't have his memories. It was easy for me to be bold.

'We need a torch,' he whispered, urgently. 'I had one somewhere, didn't I?'

'But there's a light down there, you say?'

'Yes, if it's working, there's a light. But it might not be working. And even if it is, it is deep in the cellar. It hardly lights the stairs at all.'

We looked about us for his torch. He must have left it somewhere in the hall the night that he returned from the graves, but we couldn't see it. 'What about a candle?' I suggested. 'From the dining-room.'

'Good idea.'

He went off to fetch one and returned with two, their flames spreading a kind glow in the hall.

'Take it,' he whispered. 'And this. Just in case.'

'This' was a fruit-knife from the silver-cutlery drawer in the dining-room. I didn't want it. It was sharp and lethal and too easily used.

'Are you going first or shall I?'

'I'll go first,' he agreed reluctantly, as if he wished he were a child and didn't have to.

'If I go first,' I offered, 'you can cover for me. Watch my back.' It sounded good, anyway.

'Are you sure?'

I nodded. He looked relieved. 'The door you want is just off the kitchen,' he whispered.

I waited for the tapping to resume and then crept along to the kitchen, Max breathing down my neck. As soon as we were in there, the tapping stopped. As if we had been seen. And I could feel it again immediately, that oppressive presence like a ghost haunting the room.

'This one?' I mouthed inaudibly, pointing to a door that I'd presumed was a larder door.

He nodded. I couldn't even hear him breathe any more. He waved his candle at me, then pointed at the door, and then at his eyes. I think he was saying that whoever it was had probably seen the light through the cracks around the door, which was why they had stopped the tapping noise.

I nodded. My heart was thumping so loudly in my ears, I wasn't sure that I would be able to hear the tapping anyway, if it started again.

My hands were full. I put down the knife in order to open the door. I turned the handle but the door was locked. I looked for the key in the keyhole but it wasn't there.

'On top of the architrave,' Max mouthed at me, pointing to it.

Sure enough, there it was. Exactly where it had always lived when they were children, no doubt. Too high for any of them to reach.

I put the key into the lock and was about to turn it when Max stretched in front of me to switch on the light in the cellar. It seeped dimly through the narrow space at the bottom of the door and on to the kitchen floor.

'Better to see than be seen,' he whispered.

I turned the key, grabbed my fruit-knife and stood back, side by side with Max, waiting for someone to seize their chance and throw open the door. But nothing happened.

We looked at each other. Max shook his head uncertainly and turned the key again so that the door was locked. Then he led me away from the kitchen down to the hall where he could talk without being overheard.

'It could be a trap,' he whispered.

'It feels like one.'

'We mustn't open the door.'

'But we can't *not* open the door if we want to know what it is.'

'We've got choices,' he reminded me. 'If you've been hearing that noise all this time, a few more hours won't hurt. We can wait till daylight. Or we can wait till tomorrow night when we're more prepared. We can watch – to see if it's Neil. We can . . . call the police. There's a lot we can do.'

'I'm too curious,' I said.

'Dead cat.'

'True.'

'Let's see where Laura's got to,' he suggested.

'Better switch off the light first, hadn't we?'

He looked panicky at once. 'Did we leave it on?'

'It's all right, I'll do it.'

'No. I'll do it. If anyone does it, I'll do it,' he insisted in emphatic whispers. 'I switched it on.'

I followed him back into the kitchen, although I don't think he realized. He thought he was alone. There was a false bravado to his step, as if he were trying to buoy himself up.

Then suddenly, without warning, he switched on the kitchen light and we were standing in its bright fluorescent glare, and then he was at the cellar door, turning the key without even pausing for thought, as if driven by a sudden and uncontrollable urge to see. To know. To confront whatever it was.

He pulled open the door, and I could see immediately how heavy it was, how slowly it swung, how reinforced it seemed to be. Beyond it there was nothing but darkness, pitch-black, and when Max switched the light on and off it made no difference. As if it had fused, or as if someone in the cellar had taken out the bulb. Max had blown out his candle but I still had mine. I stood beside him, holding it out in front of me through the open door. All we could see was a flight of stone steps falling away into the darkness. Nobody there.

'What now?' I whispered.

He took my candle, his hand on mine too long, too much like goodbye. 'Stay where you are,' he urged.

But I didn't. When he stepped into the darkness to shine a flame there, I followed close behind, clutching my knife for his dear life. At the bottom of the stairs there was another door with a kind of window in it, like a prison window with a shutter that you could pull up and down and pass food through. It was a very hefty door, with bolts and bars and padlocks fixed on to it. The kind of door you would use against the devil himself. But the shutter was open, as if whoever was locked in there wasn't really that dangerous after all.

Max seemed surprised by the door, as if it shouldn't be there. He held the candle up to the window to see beyond it into the cellar itself. I couldn't see what he could see at first, because he was in such a position as to mask my view. But when he gasped in such a horrified way, I moved quickly to one side of him so that my view was clear.

What I saw gave me the fright of my life, perhaps because I just wasn't expecting it. A very thin pale face stared out at me, blank as shock, framed neatly by the window. A man. Old and feeble with long white hair and a beard, more like a god than any devil, his face mottled with red blotches and scabs. I recognized the mouth, that was all; a very set mouth that nothing and nobody could touch. I didn't know that I had ever noticed it, but obviously I had. It belonged to George. It was George's mouth.

Max slammed the shutter down, as if swatting a fly. He looked at me in horror, and then pushed past me up the stairs, out into the kitchen, where I found him leaning over the table. His arms were outstretched in front of him and his head hung down between them in defeat. His breathing was exaggerated, like a man at the end of a marathon trying to contain himself.

He pulled up a chair and sat down, fixing his eyes on

a dark knot in the wood of the table, as if it would anchor him. 'Jesus,' he said. He was shaking. 'Jesus God.'

When I touched his shoulder, he jumped back with fright.

'It's OK,' I said. 'It's me.'

'I can't believe it. He's still alive. He's still fucking alive.'

His breathing was shallow now, as if the air were too thin.

'It's OK, Max. You're OK.'

'I'm not,' he contradicted. 'I'm sick to my stomach.'

'He can't hurt you any more.'

He nodded, as if to convince himself. 'I can't fucking believe it,' he said again. He hit the table with his fist. He was crying, I realized.

'He's old and weak,' I said, 'and locked behind a door.'

He nodded again, and swallowed a mouthful of air. 'What should we do?' he asked.

'Report it,' I said.

He just looked at me, that implacable expression back on his face as if it had never gone. 'Why?'

'There's nothing else we can do.'

'Isn't there?'

I could hardly answer him. I had my own confusion of impulse and reason. 'Of course not. There's only one right thing we can do,' I stated, as if I were reading it from a book. A fact, not a feeling. 'And you know it.'

'Why is it right?'

'Because we can't take the law into our own hands,' I said. 'That's what Neil has done.'

'An eye for an eye,' he said.

He wouldn't take his eyes off the knot. He traced its outline with his forefinger. 'It's come full circle,' he said.

It was very clear what he meant.

'You can't leave him down there, Max. I'm sorry.'

'It's what Jack would have done,' he retorted.

But he was wrong.

'If that's true, he'd have done it. But he didn't though, did he? He never punished George. He took it out on himself. He killed *himself*.'

A long silence. I could feel George's presence like a corpse in the room.

'He's so quiet,' whispered Max.

And then he turned to the door, where Laura was standing watching us, and he jumped with fright again. 'Fucking hell,' he said. 'How long have you been there?'

'Not long.'

Max exhaled loudly.

'He's always been quiet,' she said. She had Wren settled peacefully on her shoulder. 'From the day we put him down there.'

Max stared at her. 'Why did you do it?'

'Isn't it obvious?'

'But how? How did you get him down there?'

'The same way we almost got you down there,' she said. 'Drugs.'

He looked at her with a mixture of absolute hatred and admiration. She had done something that he would never dare to do.

'Can I have her?' I asked, reaching out for my chick.

She passed her over to me reluctantly, and then sat with us at the table. Wren snuffled a little on the journey across before falling asleep again.

'She was bawling her eyes out,' she said. 'Woke me up. I'm surprised you didn't hear.'

'Thank you.'

'It's . . . so odd . . . so ridiculous,' said Max through an almost closed mouth, his teeth grinding against each other furiously. 'All this time, and I'm still so fucking scared of him.'

He was looking at me now, as if asking me for something again, but I didn't know what, even if I could give it to him. 'You saw him. He's pathetic. I could kill him with one blow.' He was still looking at me, almost accusingly, as if I had an answer somewhere that I was withholding from him.

'I don't know, Max. I don't know why.'

'It's not physical, that's what it is. It was never physical. It's his mind, it's the way his mind works that terrifies me.'

I reached out to touch him, but he pushed my hand away. 'It's terrifying, not being able to get inside someone's head. Not being able to understand at all. Not being able to find any good reason for his cruelty.'

'I think we should report it now,' I said.

'What were you trying to do, you bitch, drugging me with that fucking port?' he shouted at Laura. He was reaching across the table, his hands at her throat.

Wren woke up and cried.

'Max, please,' I said.

'What the fuck were you doing? What the fuck were you trying to shut me in there with him for?'

'Because that way we – '

'You'll fucking pay for that. You'll be sorry you did that.'

'I'm sorry already,' she said. 'It wasn't my idea.'

'I'm going to call the police, Max,' I said. Calm as I could be.

'Wait.' He was still stretched across the table, holding on to her throat. He took his hands away very slowly, but the rest of him stayed there, a lost look in his eyes. 'Whose idea was it?' he asked. 'Yours or Neil's?'

'Partly it was Neil's, but not all of it,' she stumbled. 'You don't understand. It's not as simple as that.'

'I've got time.'

He pulled away from her altogether and sat down again. He didn't take his eyes off her.

'You can't blame Neil for everything,' she said, 'because . . . well, apart from anything else, I – I went along with it, didn't I?'

'With what?'

'With the plan. With his plan.'

'What plan?'

But she didn't explain the plan. She explained again why it was that Neil occasionally ('not *that* often') beat her up. How she definitely provoked him in many ways. How she would start the whole thing off herself sometimes, by hitting him first. In frustration. 'So it isn't all Neil,' she said.

'What was the plan, Laura?'

She looked at her bare feet in shame. 'I can't tell you.'

'You'll fucking tell me or I'll put you down there with George.'

'That's what you all say, isn't it? That's what he always says. That's what he was going to do with you, if you really want to know. Both of you. He wanted to lock Anna down there with George long before we even knew you were alive, but then she was pregnant so I wouldn't agree to it, so he threatened to put me down there too. I said I'd report him immediately. I even reached for the phone, but of course he hit me, which I suppose was understandable under the circumstances . . .'

'Oh quite understandable,' I said.

She looked irritated by my irony, but soon recovered herself. 'He was very sorry afterwards, so much so in fact that he agreed not to put you down there till you'd had the baby. We were going to keep the baby for ourselves and pretend it was ours. It was better than putting you down there with a baby, but it was still a mad idea. He said nobody would know, but – '

'I'd have known,' I said.

'Yes, but you'd have been in the cellar by then,' she said, as if that would have made me insignificant.

I began to wonder whether I was mad after all. Whether I was hallucinating. I couldn't believe that what she was saying was real.

'And you weren't getting any antenatal care down here,' she continued, 'so nobody would have bothered checking up on you, or so he thought.'

She looked at our stupefied faces.

'It was a mad idea, I agree. Completely mad. And also quite stupid really, when you think about it. I mean it's hardly as if Anna was inconspicuous in the neighbourhood, wandering around with that huge belly on her. And Drake knew she was down here. But . . .'

'But?'

'But nothing.' She went very quiet.

'If it was so mad, why did you go along with it?'

'Well, the fact was,' she said, 'we'd got away with faking George's death already, and George had got away with murdering Clarissa. So it all began to seem a lot easier.'

'How do you know?' asked Max, white as chalk.

'Know what?'

'That he murdered Clarissa?'

'Because I saw it,' she said.

'What did you see?'

'I heard them rowing – '

'What about?'

'About Neil not being George's real son.'

Max looked at me. Dread at what he was about to hear wiped across his face.

'At first he was almost tearful, as if Neil had died. He always loved Neil the best, didn't he? It was like he lived for him sometimes.'

'And then what happened?'

'Well then he went into one of his rages. Familiar to us all, I'm sure. He didn't hit her so much as swing her. He swung her by her wispy hair. And then he just hurled her down the stairs. I don't know if he really meant to kill her. It wasn't premeditated. It was just one of his rages. He was just so hurt, I think.'

'My heart bleeds for him,' said Max.

'After her death, he was a different man. Still bullying and selfish – he got worse, really, in that way – but he became so vicious towards Neil and me, it was almost like a sadist. Really vicious. We threatened to report Clarissa's death as murder if he didn't stop, so then he threatened to disinherit Neil. Well he already had, but we didn't know that. We just felt trapped in a no-win situation. We couldn't take any more of his cruelty.'

'So you started plotting his suicide?'

She hesitated. 'Yes. His murder, in fact.'

I didn't want to know any more. I felt as if Wren's sweet green shoot of life was being contaminated.

'I said no. I said I'd leave him. I got very scared. I was close anyway to leaving him, but he needs me, you see. I stop him from going too far.'

Max threw me a dry smile.

'That's why I went along with his plans. Because if I don't go along with a certain amount, he'll actually murder. Not least, he'll murder me.'

'So what happened next?' asked Max.

'Well I persuaded him that we could fake George's death, and hide him somewhere. I said I wouldn't have anything to do with actual murder.'

'So you set up his car?'

'It was so easy. Nobody even questioned it.'

'And then?'

'Neil thought of the cellar, and we put him down there. Built a new door. And then it turned out that George had changed the will already.'

'Surprise, surprise,' Max said.

'Neil was furious. He said he'd live here right under George's nose, taunt him with it for the rest of his life, serve him right.'

'And Anna was his only obstacle. Or was Jack still alive at this point?'

'Jack was still alive, yes.'

My heart thumped against my ribs.

'So did he kill Jack, then?' asked Max.

She shook her head. 'He thought Jack would make things fair, because of the way he was talking when the will was read out. He sounded so angry at the injustice of it. But then he killed himself and Anna took the lot.'

'And then I turned up,' said Max.

'That's right,' she said. 'You arrived out of nowhere. So we had to get rid of you too.'

It all sounded so practical. So methodical.

'We damn well nearly did, too. We got you nicely drugged up and brought you over here, but then we couldn't find Anna. We knew she'd start meddling if we didn't get to her soon, so we tried to trap her with you. But then she went and had that abruption.'

'So you took her to the hospital.'

'That's right. I insisted. And then Neil rushed back and put you in your bed so that you woke up without any funny suspicions – as if you'd just had a nightmare. And then we had to think what to do next.'

'Make out that I was mad.'

'Well he tried to turn it to our advantage, what had gone wrong. I told him that *he* was mad if anyone was, and to give up before he got caught, but he wasn't having it. He thought he could make out a case for you being unfit as a mother. And he nearly did, what's more.'

She was almost proud of him, you could tell. Max looked at her in horror, and then at me, for some kind of guidance. 'What do I do now?'

'Report him, Max,' I said.

He fingered the knot as if it were the whole problem, the whole imperfection, the only thing to undo. 'It's not that simple,' he muttered.

'It is from where I'm sitting,' I said.

'But he'll be a prisoner again. He's been a prisoner all his fucking life.'

'His choice,' I said.

'He was let down, Anna. By me, by Jack, by them. Is that a choice?'

'I think so. You were all let down. You didn't all act like he did.'

'You don't know a fucking thing about it though, do you?' he accused me. 'You were the apple of your parents' eyes.'

'I know one thing for sure,' I said. 'You set him an example, you and Jack. An alternative route. But he chose not to follow it. You call yourself an opportunist, Max, but I would call Neil the genuine opportunist. You left a bloody great gap for him to fill, you two, and he leapt in there, head first.'

He was trying to rub out the knot with his thumb, back and forth, wearing it down. 'The thing is,' he said, 'if I turn him in, Father will be released. He'll be out of there. He'll be walking around a free man.'

'No he won't, Max. He's a murderer.'

'Not if Laura doesn't bear witness,' he said, looking nervously at her.

'You don't have the necessary objectivity for this,' I said. 'You can't be the judge of this.'

'My father was a judge,' he retorted. 'He was the kind of judge who called a woman "provocative" when she'd been raped, or when she'd been beaten within an inch of her life. I don't trust the law.'

'I'm sorry, but I don't trust you, either. Your thinking is too devious. You have to be straight. You can't – '

'What the fuck do you know?' he almost shouted at me.

Laura was keeping very quiet.

'If it wasn't for me,' I said, 'you'd be down there now. With George.'

He glared at me.

I thought, why am I doing this? Talking about choice without exercising it? I left the room without explaining myself. I went upstairs where I couldn't be heard and telephoned the police. And then I came down again.

It wasn't until daylight, down at the police-station, that I found out who Neil's real father was. The likeness was so outstanding that I couldn't think how I had ever missed it.

Drake, it was. The spitting image of him, only Drake wore glasses and he was losing his hair.

He drove down as soon as he heard the news. It was me who told him. He wanted to act on Neil's behalf but Max intervened. And then the truth was out and he wasn't allowed even to advise Neil.

I couldn't stop staring at him.

'Perhaps if Jack had lived, and you'd struggled through a few unhappy years together with that blessed child, you'd understand it better,' he said, pointing at Wren, perceiving judgement where there was none.

'Did you know that she was murdered?' I asked.

He squinted, a strange sort of flinch that squeezed out sideways in spite of him.

'Have mercy,' said Max. 'He loved her, for God's sake.' And then he muttered under his breath, 'At least somebody did.'

Drake was polishing his spectacles with a silk handkerchief.

'Did George confess it to you?' I persisted, my mercy far away from home.

'Confess what?'

'Did he tell you that he murdered Clarissa? Or did Neil tell you?'

Max scowled at me.

'Even if there was the remotest possibility that he did murder her, which there isn't, I would never allow a client to tell me such a thing,' said Drake. 'It's not my job to keep a client's secrets. Surely you understand that.'

'I don't understand anything about this case,' I said. 'And I certainly don't understand that. She was your *lover*. He murdered her.'

'He was my client. She was my client's wife.'

'There's no point in denying it, Nicholas. We all know now. She was your lover. Neil is your son.'

'And he was my client,' Drake repeated emphatically.

'But which comes first? Love or work?'

'Work,' he said. 'Always.'

I looked at Max as one looks for shelter in a storm. This wasn't my world any more. I wondered if it was the world I might have known, had my real parents kept hold of me.

Max said, 'Leave it, Na.'

'What did you do with the money, Nicholas?' I asked, not leaving anything.

'Leave it,' Max said again.

'What money?' he asked.

'Oh, come on! George was stinking rich! Did he pay you off, was that what it was? Did you blackmail him, like Max?'

'Do you honestly believe,' he asked me in a vaguely patronizing way, 'that I would tell you, if I had done such a thing?'

And then George came floating through, the ghost of

him, chained down by handcuffs to a policeman. He looked more like a shadow than a man, thin as a prisoner of war, his footsteps so unsure that his feet seemed to touch the ground before it was there. He couldn't see very well, that was the trouble. He certainly didn't see us, although he looked our way. He was doing a strange thing with his mouth, as if he were thirsty, gulping down air. I felt a surge of pity for him, for all of them, and guilt too, as if I had been the lucky one. As if my fate had, at one stage, been identical to theirs, only God had put my mother on a bus in the nick of time and made her talk to a strange woman about babies.

Max had his arms crossed in front of him like a shield. 'He needs a drink,' he said to one of the policemen. 'Give him some water, will you?'

Neil was still being questioned somewhere in the back of the police-station. So was Laura. But it looked like George was through, for the time being, at least.

'I wonder if he's confessed,' I said.

But there was so much for him to confess, a lifetime wouldn't be long enough. I wondered how many people he had destroyed, beyond his immediate family. I was trying to concentrate on anything but Jack, that was the truth. On murder, intrigue, love, injustice, greed, you name it. Anything but the increasingly undeniable fact of his suicide. As if by killing himself he had also meant to kill me. Meant to. Had. Made the choice. It wasn't a big thing, in the context of everything else. It even looked like luck again, compared with Max's lot. But it didn't feel like luck.

I tried to think of Max instead. Tried to be some comfort to him. Took his hand in mine. He looked so bowed down, I wondered if he would ever recover. I longed for that smile to break across his face again like sun. I found myself chasing the memory of that happy summer like a compulsion, a need, wanting the hope again. Those simple expectations again. Wanting to step back over this ugly blot and start at the beginning again.

Max was gripping my hand so hard that his knuckles were white. 'I hope you love me,' he said. 'I hope you do.'

25

It wasn't a good feeling at all, giving evidence. Day after short day. Winter setting in. A hard cold edge to the air. Watching each of them shrink as I spoke. Hearing their sentences passed. It was the kind of thing you only expect to read about, while your own life passes by.

Neil got twenty-five years. Laura got ten. George got Life – what little he had left of it. Drake wasn't even tried. I don't know to this day if he was guilty of anything.

'So they all get locked up, so big deal,' muttered Max as we left. 'It still doesn't get erased from one's memory, does it?'

'Nothing does,' I said.

'It just gets stopped. The violence just gets interrupted, that's all. Nothing else goes.'

It was true. As soon as he said it, I saw Jack again in my mind's eye, dangling in the empty heart of the stair-well like a doll. Nothing new. I saw him there most days. After a while it stopped catching my breath and just became a part of my day, my scenery, as if I'd got used to it. Like Max had got used to the way his childhood was.

But in fact you never get used to those things. Those peculiar things. They set you apart.

I linked arms with him as we walked down the corridor. We were coming out of the court-room. Drake was ahead of us, showing no feeling. His step was light and his face was composed as he turned round to say goodbye. 'I hope your daughter is thriving?' he asked.

'She is, thank you. She's with Mum at the moment. I think she's sensed the strain a bit, but – '

'No doubt,' he conceded. 'Who hasn't?'

There was a tiny hint of distress around his mouth which he covered with his hand. I had the feeling that he was falling apart in there.

'Your family must have found it hard too,' I ventured.

'We've all found it hard,' he said quickly. 'Haven't we? It's not the kind of thing one takes blithely in one's stride.'

He was looking at the ground, talking as fast as ever. He seemed always to find communication a distasteful but necessary inconvenience. 'Goodbye,' he said, looking up from the ground very suddenly, hand outstretched. He shook Max's hand first, then mine. And then he turned round and walked away, almost breaking into a run.

We followed his path far more slowly, held up by too much thought.

'We must try to put this right behind us, all the same,' said Max. 'Not deny it, I don't mean that. I've tried doing that.'

He stopped walking altogether. He had me hanging on one arm, and his overcoat on the other. He picked at the coat where the thread was bare. 'I don't want to pretend that they don't exist any more. I'll visit them regularly. Get to know who they are.'

I thought, that's what I'll do too. Find my mother. Get to know who she is. Maybe even find my father somewhere.

'But we must start building a different life too, a new

life,' he said. 'New memories. If we can just do something happy every day for the next forty years, we'll put this so far behind us that it won't hurt any more.' He paused briefly. 'Agreed?'

'Agreed.'

He turned to look at me. '*Do* you love me?' he asked, worry troubling his brow so ferociously that I feared he might not want me to.

'Oh I do, yes,' I said, apologetically. 'Is that all right?'

He started walking again, looking straight ahead while I scanned his face for evidence of some mutual feeling for me. A smile spread so slowly across his face that I wasn't sure what it was, whether it was pity or love.

'I really do, Max. I always have,' I said.

And then suddenly his smile spread everywhere, right across his face, like something he couldn't contain. He turned round and picked me up and spun me in the air. 'Fuck it!' he said. 'Let's start!'

We ran the rest of the way, into the high hall and out on to the steps. It was raining heavily outside. The wind was scuffing up the fallen leaves like confetti, billowing umbrellas inside out. Coats and skirts all swirled about in a flamboyant dance that wouldn't be held down. We stood arm in arm beneath the sheltering porch of the court. Max put up his own umbrella and it shot out in front of him, dragging us both into the dance with the rest of them. He was laughing the way he always used to laugh, the way I loved him to laugh, his wet hair clutching at his face like tendrils. And I was happy too, I really was, I was laughing too, you couldn't *not* laugh when Max laughed, but I kept thinking of Jack, of his smile too, his laughter, his love.

'I have to do something today,' I said, pulling at Max's sleeve. 'Listen to me, Max; I have to do something.'

'You have to be happy today,' he said.

'I *am* happy,' I said. 'But I have to scatter Jack.'

'What?' He stopped spinning in the rain and leaned in close to me. 'What did you say?'

'Jack,' I said. 'I have to scatter him.'

He looked very serious. 'Scatter him?'

'His ashes.'

'Oh. I see.' He frowned. 'Haven't you scattered them yet?'

I didn't like his tone. 'There's no right time to throw someone away.'

'No,' he agreed. 'Of course not.'

He didn't show it, but I think he was laughing inside.

Maybe it was funny.

26

I didn't scatter Jack that day. I thought he might like a last word with George, so I took him to prison with me in my bag, like a trophy. Victory over so much. I wanted to put him under George's nose and say: see how you killed him too. But when it came to it, I couldn't even bring myself to take him out of my bag. I couldn't rub George's nose in the dust that was his son, whether he was sorry or not. Apart from anything else, I couldn't put Jack through that.

I had the feeling that Jack was impatient now, keen to be free of me, almost looking forward to his scattering. As if three was a crowd.

It was hard to give him up.

I was scared of George. I had seen how Max was with him. When I was sitting opposite him, two days after his trial, my heart was in my mouth.

He looked respectable again, the way he had looked in court. Clean-shaven, his white hair cut short and combed back so that you could see where the teeth had been. His face was filling out a little with prison food, but it was still an angular face. Sharp wherever it could be. Hollow around the eyes and cheeks.

'I have some questions to ask you,' I said.

He didn't respond. I could hear my blood as it pumped fast through my veins.

'Why do you think Jack killed himself?'

'Because he was weak,' he said, without even thinking about it.

I had to pinch myself.

'Weak? In what way?'

'I'm surprised you have to ask.'

'I do,' I said. 'I didn't know him as weak. I always saw him as brave.'

He had the nerve to laugh. 'He was essentially destructive, Jack. You must have discovered that? He didn't know how to build anything, did he? He only knew how to destroy.'

'No,' I said. 'I didn't discover that.'

'Well if you didn't *then*, you have *now*,' he said. 'Too late. Bad luck.'

I said, 'You don't see yourself as responsible in any way for his destructiveness?'

'Good Lord, no. That would be extremely arrogant, wouldn't it?'

'Or extremely humble,' I suggested.

'I'm not God,' he said. 'I don't make people what they are.'

'But you must have had some influence over your children, surely?'

'It doesn't appear so.' He reflected. 'A little, perhaps.'

'Do you believe that human beings influence each other at all?'

'Not entirely. I think we are born the way we are, on the whole.'

'That's bleak,' I said.

'Call it that if you like.'

'What do you call it?'

'Realistic.' Pause. 'I hope you haven't got a tape-recorder running in that bag?'

Of sorts, I thought.

'No, I haven't.'

'Because it feels like a bloody interview, this.'

'Would you say that you were a cruel father?'

'I was a strict father, not cruel. Children need discipline, as I'm sure you'll agree.'

'But you picked on Jack, didn't you?'

'Because he asked for it.'

'How?'

'He was extremely disrespectful as a boy. He had to be taught a lesson.'

'And were you respectful of him?'

He looked at me for a moment in disbelief.

'Were you?'

'Oh for goodness sake!' he laughed. 'What a question!'

'Is it so funny?'

'It's more than funny. It's ridiculous.'

'Why?'

He shook his head at me.

'Would you call yourself a bully, George?'

'What sort of question is that?'

'Your children would.'

His face became dangerous. I knew the signs now. It did the same thing that Neil's face had done.

'When I was a teenager,' I said, brave because I was safe, 'I watched you hit your wife across the face. You didn't know I was there. I was so shocked, I thought I must have misinterpreted it. But now I realize that it was nothing for either of you, that. A mere – '

'I think I've had enough of this unsolicited visit,' he said.

'You killed Jack, really, didn't you?'

'What?'

'You're the great destroyer, not him.'

'I killed my wife. Isn't that enough to lay at my door?'

'But you broke his spirit, didn't you?'

His eyes were cold, still as glass, transfixing me. 'I'm not taking responsibility for my son's weaknesses. I've enough of my own.'

He was silent. I thought that if he would only show some remorse, I might even pity him. But his pride was immense, unappealing as a mountain to climb at the end of a long road.

'What was your own childhood like?' I asked.

'Disciplined.'

'You got locked in cellars too, did you?'

'Not cellars, no.' His mouth puckered up the way Neil's would.

'Were you beaten?'

He stood up, his chair scraping on the floor behind him. 'Come and talk to me when you're grown up,' he said. 'When your own child is old enough to answer back at you.'

'Please – don't go yet,' I said, fingering Jack's urn in my bag.

He leaned across the table towards me, the way Max had leaned towards Laura that night, hands at her throat. 'Listen,' he said. 'I was a judge for twenty-five years. I wasn't as fair as I might have been, but I did my best. I saw a lot of evil in that time, and I had to judge it, however inadequately. Who should I have punished? The criminal? Or his father?'

He stood up to his full height, as if it symbolized his moral stature somehow. He looked as if he had said something indisputable. In fact he had said something general in answer to a very specific and personal question.

I said, 'If a small child stabs himself with a sharp knife, who do I blame? The child? Or his father?'

'Jack was a grown man when he took his life,' he said.

'But he'd been taking his life all his life! For as long as he had it. He was always doing it. He did it every time he answered back at your injustice, George.'

'How dare you,' he said. His voice was too concentrated, as if it needed watering down. 'How *dare* you come here with your childish accusations and hurl them in my face. Wait until your own children turn round and thank you for feeding them and clothing them.'

'And loving them,' I said.

But he turned and walked away without even hearing me.

I couldn't move for some time. It was as if he had snowed me under with his contempt. So that I couldn't hear myself. So that I doubted myself. As if I might have wronged him, after all. It wasn't until much later, recounting it to Max, that I remembered he was a murderer.

Epilogue

I had to hire a balloon in the end to fulfil Jack's request. I couldn't get close enough to the sky – to my heaven, as he called it – no matter how high I climbed. Or maybe it was just that I couldn't get far enough away from the earth.

I thought about taking Wren, but I worried about her ears. Whether they would pop too much. And also, I felt that if I took her and left Max behind, I'd be excluding him, which didn't feel right. So I left them both behind, in each other's capable hands.

It was a memorable day. Perhaps not happy in the way that Max meant, but it was sweet enough, in its own melancholic way. Just me and Jack and Jack's Leica and a man I didn't know, floating over the sea. It had to be the sea, in case the camera hit someone on dry land.

Before I threw the camera I opened it, to check there was no film inside. Two small photographs fell out. They looked as if they had been selected from a contact print. They were both of Jack, and they were both so under-exposed that I could hardly make them out. I knew instantly that one of them at least was the photograph with which he had been so preoccupied in the last days of his life, and I was right that it was a clue. They were both clues. On the back of one he had scribbled *Is this me?* and on the other, *Or is this?*

They looked like self-portraits rather than someone else's work, judging from the angle. It was his favourite angle, as good as a signature. I thought I could see that he was smiling in one, while in the other he looked sad. More than sad, he looked. Deeply unhappy. I don't know how I could tell, really; they just looked like two shadowy images with writing on the back. Maybe I endowed them with my own meaning, because I needed to. Or maybe I just knew him well enough to tell. I thought they were his answer to Jeff Shue's portrait of him. To that whole irritating exhibition, in fact. That faces can hide whatever they want to hide. That you have to really want to see the truth to find it there.

I leaned over the side of the basket and let him go.

Ashes, first. A sudden dissolving cloud that used to be his life.

Camera, second. A small drop falling soundlessly into the ocean.

Photographs, last. Fluttering like freed birds.